All she needed was one opportunity to get away

Keeping one eye on her, Ben opened the driver's side door of the rental car, clipped his gun into his belt and said, "Okay, get in."

Monique slid under the wheel and across to the passenger's side, watching him from the corner of her eye. He climbed in after her, then turned his head toward the door as he closed it.

Seizing the moment, she dived for her own door. She had her fingers on the handle when he caught her—one hand digging into her shoulder, the other grabbing her head.

As he jerked her backward, her glasses went flying and her wig came off in his hand. As her hair fell free around her shoulders, Ben DeCarlo's eyes tuned to icy blue steel.

"Damn!" he muttered. "Of all the women in the world, I grabbed Monique LaRoquette. Witness for the prosecution."

Dear Reader,

I'm so glad you've decided to pick up
The Valentine Hostage, the last book of three in
the exciting miniseries EYEWITNESS. If you missed
them, I hope you'll also look for *A Christmas Kiss*
by Caroline Burnes, which was out in December,
and *A New Year's Conviction* by Cassie Miles,
which was out in January.

The most common question readers ask me is,
"Where do you get your ideas?" That's sometimes
difficult to say, because I don't always know. For
many of my books, it seemed as if the idea was
just floating in the air and drifted into my brain
osmosis-like.

In the case of *The Valentine Hostage*, though, I
know exactly where the idea came from. I
answered my phone one day and my editor said,
"I'd like to see a miniseries featuring people in the
Witness Protection Program. Are you interested?"

After playing a little "what if," we decided it would
be neat to do three stories about witnesses to the
same double murder. They've been in the Witness
Protection Program since they testified at the
killer's trial, and the EYEWITNESS books tell what
happens when the murderer is granted a retrial
and the witnesses are expected to testify again.

I really enjoyed writing a story set in romantic
New Orleans and the Louisiana bayou country, so
I hope you enjoy reading it.

Warmest regards,

Dawn Stewardson

The Valentine Hostage
Dawn Stewardson

Harlequin Books

TORONTO • NEW YORK • LONDON
AMSTERDAM • PARIS • SYDNEY • HAMBURG
STOCKHOLM • ATHENS • TOKYO • MILAN
MADRID • WARSAW • BUDAPEST • AUCKLAND

To Cheryl Smith, with thanks for the generosity of her ideas. To constables Sue MacDonell and Steven Charlton, who help with the "cop stuff"—and never really charge the $50 an hour they threaten me with.

And to John, always.

ISBN 0-373-22406-0

THE VALENTINE HOSTAGE

Copyright © 1997 by Dawn Stewardson

This edition published by arrangement with Harlequin Books S.A.

® and TM are trademarks of the publisher. Trademarks indicated with ® are registered in the United States Patent and Trademark Office, the Canadian Trade Marks Office and in other countries.

Printed in U.S.A.

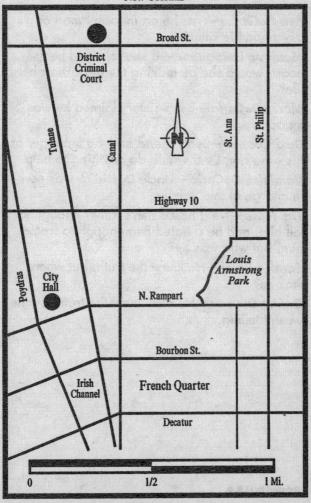

New Orleans

Broad St.

District Criminal Court

Tulane

Canal

St. Ann

St. Philip

N

Highway 10

Louis Armstrong Park

Poydras

City Hall

N. Rampart

Bourbon St.

Irish Channel

French Quarter

Decatur

0   1/2   1 Mi.

CAST OF CHARACTERS

Ben DeCarlo—Was he an innocent man or a psychopathic killer?

Monique LaRoquette—If she followed her heart, would she be making the mistake of her life?

Maria DeCarlo—Ben's sister claimed he was innocent.

Dezi Cooper—Ben's friend and the manager of his wine bar, Dezi would do anything to help.

Dominick DeCarlo—Uncle Dominick was now in charge of the "family."

The Nose—He'd hated Ben's father enough to kill him, and he'd hated Ben enough to frame him, but who was he?

Sandor Rossi—He knew the truth, but where was he?

Danny Dupray—He also knew the truth, but he wasn't telling.

Prologue

The minute they walked into Augustine's, Monique was glad she'd opted to have lunch with Frankie, rather than the other models. It was obvious he'd been right, that the café-bar *was* one of the must places to visit in New Orleans. The long, dim room, with its stone floor, murmuring ceiling fans and muted lighting, positively oozed atmosphere.

"That was a great shoot this morning," Frankie said once they'd been shown to a table. "If they gave Pulitzers for fashion photography, I'd be clearing a space on my mantel when we get back to New York."

Monique smiled. "You know, I'm tempted never to *go* back. Two days and I've fallen in love with this city."

"You should see it at Mardi Gras. That's enough to blow your mind. But the most you can hope for is a trip here now and then. You're one of the lucky ones who look younger all the time, so you'll be stuck working in New York for another twenty years."

"Oh, you're *such* a silver-tongued devil, Frankie."

He laughed at that. Then, before he said anything more, a waitress arrived with menus.

While Frankie began to peruse his, Monique glanced slowly around the restaurant, thinking she really *was* one of the lucky ones.

Modeling was a tough business that saw a lot of women over the hill well before they hit thirty. But, at twenty-eight, she was still landing assignments with the major magazines. And older models were getting more and more work as the population aged, which augured well for at least her immediate future.

Yes, she had the world by the tail, as her mother was fond of pointing out. A successful career and a good man back home who wanted to marry her. So even though she wasn't *entirely* sure that Craig was Mr. Right...

Her thoughts of him trailed off when the door opened, drawing her attention to the man who strode into Augustine's. If *he* wasn't somebody's Mr. Right, she'd be awfully surprised. He was about thirty, tall and nicely built, with sun-streaked brown hair and a sexy cleft in his chin.

He had definite presence, his designer overcoat said *money*, and he'd be attractive as all get-out if it weren't for the scowl on his face.

"Hey," Frankie said quietly, "he sure looks like an unhappy camper, huh?"

The man surveyed the restaurant for another second, then started toward the back.

As he did, a woman said, "Why, there's Ben."

Glancing around to see who knew him, Monique discovered it was an older couple at a table in the back corner. The woman was elegance personified, wearing a Gianni Versace suit of winter white wool. The man bore a passing resemblance to Anthony Quinn.

"Ben," he said, half rising. "Come and have lunch with us, son."

The woman began to speak again, then her words faded and her expression grew uncertain.

Monique looked at the younger man once more. He'd stopped several feet from the couple, and just as she turned toward him he pulled a handgun from beneath his coat.

"Oh, jeez!" Frankie whispered. "Get down!"

He dove for the floor, but Monique sat frozen where she was. Above the pounding in her ears, she could hear the man with the gun angrily saying something about not running for the Senate, something about the older man interfering in his life.

Then two shots rang out and the man at the table fell backward. The woman slumped against the wall, hemorrhaging from her throat, the blood turning her winter white jacket scarlet.

For a horrified moment, Monique watched—until a wave of nausea and blood-black color swept in front of her eyes and total blackness engulfed her.

Chapter One

Monday, February 3, 1997
3:01 p.m.

When the news came on Monique was in the spare bedroom she used as a home office—checking her computer for the most recent house listings and telling herself that sooner or later she'd turn up something to fit the Ramseys' requirements.

"This hour's top story comes from our sister station in New Orleans," the announcer said.

Monique looked at the radio.

"One of the most publicized trials in that city's history, the retrial of Ben DeCarlo on two counts of murder, has just ended."

The words grabbed her complete attention. Ever since the witness protection people had flown her to New Orleans last month, to testify for the prosecution a second time, those murders had been almost constantly on her mind.

Aside from anything else, it was hard to stop thinking about something that seemed to be referred to on every newscast and in each day's newspaper. So thank heavens the trial was over.

"Earlier today," the announcer continued, "the defense team rested its case. And only minutes ago, the two sides completed their closing statements. The jury will be charged tomorrow morning.

"This brings to an end a retrial that many people feel should never have been granted. In late 1994, the original trial for the murder of alleged crime lord Antonio DeCarlo and his wife, five eyewitnesses testified to seeing Ben DeCarlo walk into a New Orleans restaurant and gun down his parents. Their testimonies convicted him."

Alleged crime lord, Monique silently repeated. There was nothing *alleged* about it. Antonio DeCarlo had been head of a *major* New Orleans crime family.

"But after spending two years in the Louisiana State Prison at Angola," the announcer went on, "DeCarlo was granted a retrial on the basis of new evidence. Evidence which failed to materialize during the trial. Evidence some people doubt ever existed.

"Many of those same people believe DeCarlo was behind the recent murders of two of the five eyewitnesses, but only time will tell whether their killers have links to DeCarlo."

Closing her eyes, Monique wondered how anyone could doubt Ben DeCarlo had arranged for those killings.

Oh, she knew some people in New Orleans claimed he'd never had anything to do with the Dixie Mafia. That despite his father's activities, Ben had been a law-abiding businessman.

But she didn't believe it for a minute. She'd seen him murder his parents, and no one went from law-abiding citizen to cold-blooded killer in the blink of an eye.

"So," the announcer was saying, "the retrial is over except for the verdict. And it is expected to come quickly. Speculation has it the jury deliberations may set a record for brevity.

"Turning to other news…"

Monique exhaled slowly, only then aware she'd been holding her breath. She hadn't realized *quite* how anxiously she'd been waiting to hear that the trial was finished.

But testifying again had brought back all her vivid images of those murders, and maybe now they'd begin to fade. Hopefully, the nightmares that had returned to plague her would gradually go away, as well.

Because unless something went dreadfully wrong in the jury room, Benjamin Wilson DeCarlo would be found guilty of those murders this time, too. And she knew it would do a lot to lower her anxiety level.

She looked at the phone—flirting with the idea of being in that courtroom when the verdict was read. Then she told herself to resist temptation.

If she wanted to remain in the witness protection program, she was supposed to do what she was told. And she'd been told to stay out of New Orleans for the rest of her life.

The Big Easy was where Ben DeCarlo's friends were. The friends who'd already murdered two of the five eyewitnesses.

Thinking about the two men brought tears to her eyes—and sent a shiver through her. Both of them had been in the witness protection program, like her, but now they were dead. And that made her certain she'd never be truly safe. Even though the trial was over, Ben DeCarlo might still have her killed to prove he had connections, even from a prison cell. Or as revenge. Or simply because criminals lived in a different world which ran by its own rules.

But even though she knew that going to New Orleans wouldn't be wise, she needed closure. Wanted to see firsthand that Ben DeCarlo was found guilty again.

Assuming he *would* be. Assuming something *didn't* go wrong in the jury room.

Firmly, she assured herself nothing would. After the defense team's key witness had mysteriously developed amnesia, the news pundits had been predicting that not only would the jurors find Ben DeCarlo guilty, they'd also take less than a full day to deliberate.

She thought about that for a minute, glancing at her date book to be certain she had no upcoming appointments she couldn't reschedule.

Of course, real estate agents were supposed to be on call practically twenty-four hours a day. And there was no *guarantee* those jurors would set a record for brevity.

But she could pack enough clothes to get her through a few days—just in case. And she could leave word at her office that there was an emergency in her family. That she had to go to spend a few days with her parents and wasn't sure exactly when she'd be back.

Looking at the photograph on her desk, she wished with all her heart that she *could* spend some time with them. And with her brother. Because of Ben DeCarlo, though, she was obliged to live a lie, cut off from her former life, calling herself Anne Gault rather than Monique LaRoquette.

But things were the way things were, and she'd learned not to sit around feeling sorry for herself. So she turned her thoughts back to the question at hand.

Her years of modeling had taught her how to drastically alter her appearance. And if no one could possibly recognize her, would a brief visit to New Orleans really be dangerous?

Making her decision, she picked up the phone.

Tuesday, February 4
11:24 a.m.

MONIQUE SAT WITH HER hands pressed tightly together as the jurors filed back into the courtroom. They'd taken scarcely two hours to deliberate Benjamin Wilson DeCarlo's fate, and in another few moments she'd know for certain what it was.

If they'd voted to set him free, though, she didn't know whether she could bear it.

Because of him, people were dead. His parents. The witnesses he'd had killed.

Because of him, she was living a lonely lie. He'd taken everything from her—her family, her career, even her husband. And for all of that, she hated Ben DeCarlo from the depths of her soul.

"Ladies and gentlemen of the jury," the judge said once they were seated, "have you reached a verdict?"

"We have, Your Honor," the foreman told him, handing a folded sheet of paper to the court clerk.

The clerk delivered the verdict to the judge.

From the last row of the courtroom, Monique watched his face while he read it, searching for any trace of a reaction. There wasn't a flicker.

As he began refolding the paper, she smoothed a few stray hairs on the Cleopatra-type wig she was wearing, and uneasily adjusted the eye glasses that added to her disguise. Then she focused on the jury once more.

The court officer had delivered the verdict back to the foreman, and the room was so quiet that even from where she was sitting she could hear the faint crackle as he unfolded the paper.

This was the moment she'd been waiting for, and she turned her gaze to the accused. To the man who'd gunned down his own parents in Augustine's.

He was sitting with his cuffed hands on the table in front of him, looking intently at the jurors, which meant that from her aisle seat his profile was clearly visible. Fleetingly, she recalled how attractive she'd thought he was when he'd walked into the restaurant that day.

So much for first impressions. Now, watching him, she saw nothing but a cold, calculating murderer.

"Your Honor," the foreman read, "we find the defendant guilty as charged."

For all the apparent effect that verdict had on Ben DeCarlo, his handsome face might have been chiseled from stone.

But it was typical for a psychopath to show no emotion. And there was little doubt that's what he was. One of the prosecution's expert witnesses had been an eminent psychiatrist, and he'd testified that only a psychopath could have killed his parents in cold blood the way Ben DeCarlo had.

She looked away from him and leaned back, feeling relieved that justice had been served a second time, that Ben DeCarlo would never be a free man. But she also felt strangely hollow. The sense of satisfaction she'd anticipated wasn't there.

Perhaps that was because Ben DeCarlo was evil incarnate. Which meant he'd only gotten what he deserved.

She watched the two armed guards lead him from the courtroom, thinking that now the verdict was in, she wanted nothing more than to catch the next flight back to Hartford, Connecticut.

BEN DECARLO WALKED out of the courtroom between the guards, his adrenaline pumping like crazy. It was now or never. Prisoners didn't escape from Angola, so if this plan failed...

If this plan failed, he'd rather be dead than back in prison. And he was sure he'd have no trouble getting either of these armed guards to grant that wish.

While one of them closed the courtroom door, Ben stared down the long hallway, wishing he could see around the corner at the end.

What if his guys weren't waiting there? What if something had gone wrong or someone had double-crossed him?

Nothing had gone wrong, he told himself as they started down the hall. The men they'd hired were pros who would do precisely what they'd been paid to do. They were the best money could buy.

As for his sister and his buddy, Dezi, he could only thank God they'd stuck by him through all this. And he'd trust them with his life. Hell, he *was* trusting them with it.

"Guess you're lookin' forward to seein' all your convict friends again, huh, DeCarlo?" one of the guards said. "I hear Angola's a real fun place to live. You musta missed it durin' your trial."

Ben didn't even glance in the guard's direction, but he could hear the smirk on the guy's face. Angola made hell look like a vacation resort.

They'd almost reached the end of the hallway, and with each step Ben's heart was beating harder. This was so well planned it *had* to work. He couldn't know the layout of the building better if there was a floor plan etched in his brain—he knew exactly where to go, exactly what to do.

Then they were at the corner…making the turn to the right.…

"What the—"

A fresh wave of adrenaline surged through him as his men went into action. Two of them were taking care of the guards—slapping duct tape across their mouths. Tying their hands behind their backs. The third one unlocked Ben's handcuffs, then shoved a gym bag at him and silently pointed toward the far end of the hall.

He didn't need directions. He took off running, unzipping the bag as he went.

Wheeling into the washroom, he dug through the bag, pulling out everything he needed right away. Then he ripped off his suit jacket and tugged the gray sweater on over his shirt.

His hands trembling, he peeled the backing off the fake mustache. Peering into the mirror, he firmly pressed it on.

After pulling the baseball cap down low enough to hide the front of his hair, he shoved the wallet into his pocket and put on the dark sunglasses. Finally, he clipped the Walther .38 to his belt and pulled the sweater loosely over it.

He was out of the washroom again before he'd even finished stuffing his jacket and tie into the bag.

A quick glance to his left assured him his men were gone, their job was done. The guards had been safely locked in the storage room.

"*Ciao,* fellows," he said under his breath. Then he headed for the rarely used exit he knew had been unlocked for him.

Once outside, he forced himself to walk along the alley next to the courthouse at a normal pace, even though he wanted to run flat out.

So far, everything had gone like clockwork. And that was because they'd thought through every detail carefully. Which meant he couldn't deviate from the plan. He had to walk, not run and attract attention.

But it would be only a matter of minutes, maybe

even seconds, before someone realized he'd escaped. And he sure didn't want to be hanging around when all hell broke loose.

Reaching the street, he looked quickly in either direction—and realized she wasn't there.

Trying to ignore the fingers of panic that wrapped themselves around his throat, he checked again, gazing along the block more slowly this time. She had to be *some*where.

No car, they'd decided. No license plate that someone might remember. A taxi would be better. But a taxi for him *and* Felicia, the woman they'd paid to be here.

He looked one more time, but the only woman standing alone on the sidewalk wasn't Felicia. This one was wearing a pale yellow suit, not the dark slacks and a green sweater he'd been expecting. Plus, she had a coat draped over her arm, was holding a small suitcase and wasn't standing in their designated spot.

He stared at her, willing her to metamorphose into Felicia. It didn't happen. Her straight black hair and glasses didn't vanish. And no matter how hard he stared, she looked nothing like the picture they'd shown him.

He took a final, futile look up and down the street, then glanced back at the woman in the yellow suit— those fingers of panic growing tighter and tighter around his throat.

He had to have a woman. That was critical to their plan.

THE DAY WAS WARM for February, almost seventy, and after spending her morning in the stuffy courthouse Monique paused for a few breaths of fresh air, hoping they'd drive at least some of the thoughts of Ben DeCarlo from her mind.

When they didn't, she tried concentrating on the hustle and bustle around her.

The street was filled with people, many of them obviously tourists—the cameras around their necks a dead giveaway. The cabbie who'd driven her in from the airport had been a nonstop talker, so she knew Mardi Gras was early this year, a week from today, to be exact. And the Carnival celebrations already had people pouring into the city.

Across the street, a hot dog vendor was doing brisk business at his Lucky Dog cart, which made her wonder if she should grab something from him. She'd rarely had a good experience with airport food.

On the other hand, there was a flight leaving for Hartford in a couple of hours, and if she wanted to get booked onto it she should probably just hail a cab and worry about food later.

She glanced along the street, looking for an empty one—and saw something that turned her blood to ice water. Ben DeCarlo was standing not twenty feet away.

For a few panicked seconds, she was so frightened her brain stopped working. Then she realized it couldn't possibly be him. Only minutes ago, he'd been led out of the courtroom wearing a charcoal Armani suit. The man down the street had on a blue sweatshirt, jeans and cowboy boots.

Staring at him, she searched for telltale differences. But he was so much like Ben DeCarlo that—

"Don't move a muscle," a man whispered, placing a hand firmly on her arm.

Startled, she turned and looked at him. For a moment, she didn't realize who he was. Then her eyes were drawn to the cleft in his chin, and the sunglasses and mustache might as well have vanished from his face.

"Oh, God," she murmured, her startled feeling escalating into pure terror. The man down the street wasn't Ben DeCarlo, but the man with his hand on her arm was.

She tried telling herself her eyes were playing tricks on her, but they weren't.

He had on a gray sweater, now, instead of his suit jacket, and a baseball cap pulled low over his face, hiding his sunstreaked hair. But he was still wearing the charcoal Armani suit pants and the expensive Italian shoes.

"I have a gun," he said, the gentleness of his Southern accent not right for the words he was saying. "And if you scream or try to get away, I'll use it."

She stood rooted to the spot, gripping the handle of her suitcase so tightly her fingernails began to dig into her palms. Her heart was beating triple time, her mouth felt cotton dry, and her throat was so tight she couldn't swallow.

Her deepest darkest fear had just become reality. Ben DeCarlo had escaped. And whether she screamed or tried to escape or stood stock-still, he'd kill her. There wasn't the slightest doubt in her mind.

"Now, here's what's going to happen," he said, setting the sports bag he'd been holding onto the sidewalk. "I'm going to hail a cab and we'll get into it. And you just keep quiet. If there's anything you *have* to say to me, pretend I'm your husband. Understand?"

Wordlessly, Monique nodded, a fresh wave of terror sweeping her. Being taken hostage by a psychopathic murderer might prove even worse than being killed on the spot.

She knew the sorts of things psychopaths were capable of. She'd read a lot about them, trying to understand how Ben DeCarlo could possibly have done what he had.

"Okay," he said, "let's get this show on the road." He barely raised his arm before a cabbie cut across a lane toward them.

"I'm not going to hurt you," he whispered, picking up the sports bag as the taxi pulled to a halt. "Not as long as you do what I say. But don't forget for a second that I've got a gun."

And he has nothing to lose, added a voice inside Monique's head.

Ben followed the woman into the back of the taxi, his heart pounding harder than a jackhammer. It wasn't like him to panic, but that was certainly what he'd done when he'd realized Felicia hadn't shown.

He'd practically been able to see his freedom being snatched from him once again. So even though he didn't know if he was doing the smart thing by hijacking this stranger, he wasn't in any position to stand around debating the pros and cons with himself.

Any moment now, there'd be an APB out and all the heat in New Orleans would be looking for him. But they'd be looking for a man alone, which meant he had a far better chance of getting completely away if he was with a woman.

Besides that, if he didn't have one when he got to the airport, the plan could well run into a snag. So he wasn't going to worry, right now, about the problems he'd created by grabbing her.

"Where to?" the cabbie asked, pulling away from the curb.

"New Orleans International," Ben told him, thinking it was a lucky break the woman had a suitcase. They'd worried he'd get the sort of cabbie who'd remember a fare to the airport with only a gym bag for luggage.

But they'd decided that even if the guy *did* remember picking up someone outside the courthouse, even if he *did* eventually realize it might have been a disguised Ben DeCarlo, what better destination for the cops to learn about than New Orleans International?

If they figured that had been his first stop, they'd assume his second was South America or some other far-flung place.

Leaning back against the seat, he tried to relax a little. He was far too wired, though, and would be until he got where he was going. But at least he was starting to think straight again. Which meant he'd better give some thought to the woman. Decide what the hell he was going to do with her.

He glanced at her sitting stiffly next to him, staring straight ahead. She was clearly terrified.

Of course, that was hardly surprising. And if she knew he was Ben DeCarlo, she'd be even more frightened.

Eying her, he had the feeling he'd seen her someplace before. But that would be just too much of a coincidence.

Looking out as they turned onto Tulane, he tried to decide whether it would be safe to let her go once he was finished at the airport.

The last thing he wanted was to take her with him. That wasn't part of the plan any more than grabbing her had been. But if he let her go she'd call the heat. Even though she didn't know who he was, he'd shanghaied her right in front of the courthouse. So the cops would put two and two together. Fast. And it would be far, far better if they had nothing at all.

Glancing at her again, he weighed in another factor. No matter how briefly he held her hostage, he was already guilty of kidnapping. Which, under the law, was almost as serious as murder.

Chapter Two

"Where ya'll wanna be dropped?" the cabbie asked as they neared the terminal.

"International departures," Ben DeCarlo said.

The knot in Monique's stomach began to ache. The only possible reason he'd forced her to come with him was that he'd seen right through her disguise and intended to kill her as revenge for testifying against him.

And if he was leaving the country, she didn't have long to live. He'd have a passport for himself, but he'd hardly have one for her, so she'd be dead before he got on his plane.

While the taxi was pulling to a stop, she told herself there had to be at least a chance she could escape from this alive. No matter how badly he wanted to kill her, he might not have a good opportunity. Not in an airport full of people.

That logic did little to calm her fears. After all, he'd murdered his parents in a crowded restaurant.

He handed some bills to the cabbie, then grabbed her right hand firmly in his left. Clutching her suitcase, she slid across the seat after him.

Once they were inside the terminal, he said, "Give me your coat."

When she handed it to him, he draped it over his arm, glanced around, then reached beneath his sweater. Nonchalantly, he slid the trench coat over his hand as he brought it back out—but not nonchalantly enough that she didn't realize he was holding his gun now.

That made her throat go so dry that when he said, "What's your name?" she couldn't answer immediately.

She simply stared at him, her thoughts racing as rapidly as her pulse. She'd been wrong. He *hadn't* seen through her disguise.

"Anne," she finally said, a tiny spark of hope flickering in her heart. If he didn't know who she was, things might not be quite as bad as she'd thought.

"Okay, Anne, for the next little while, you're Mary Carson of Silver Bay, Minnesota. I've got a driver's license for you, and a credit card. I want you to sign both of them as Mary Carson. Then we'll walk along to that rental counter. There's a car reserved in Mary's name."

Oh, Lord. He wasn't leaving the country at all. Which meant he could keep her with him for as long as he liked.

He dug the cards and a pen from his sports bag and handed them to her. She shakily signed them, her mind racing again. If he'd only made her come with him to rent a car, maybe when she'd done that...

"Good," he said once she'd finished signing. "Now, I'll be right beside you while you're talking to the clerk. So don't get any funny ideas."

After taking a deep breath, she said, "If I do this for you, you'll let me go?"

"Yes, but not here where you can run to a phone."

"What if I promise I won't?"

"That's not good enough. You'll have to stick with me for the time being."

Despite her fear, she stood her ground when he motioned her to start off. *The time being* would undoubtedly prove long enough for him to realize who she really was. And once he knew, he'd kill her for sure. So if she was going to end up dead, anyway, why should she cooperate?

It took him mere seconds to convince her she'd better. He moved menacingly close and gave her a glimpse of the gun.

That was more effective than words would have been. Effective enough that she walked directly along to the car rental counter with him.

She made it through dealing with the clerk, even managing a smile when he informed her the Chevy Caprice he was giving her was "brand, spanking new."

Then, once she'd signed Mary Carson's name in three different places, he handed her a set of car keys and gave her directions to the parking lot.

"Let's go," Ben said.

Walking away from the counter, she told herself

not to give up hope. All she needed was one opportunity to get away. Silently, she repeated the words like a mantra—over and over again until they reached the blue Caprice.

Keeping one eye on her, Ben unlocked the trunk, tossed his sports bag and her coat into it and motioned her to do the same with her suitcase. Then he opened the driver's side door, clipped the gun to his belt and said, "Okay, get in."

She slid under the wheel and across to the passenger's side, all the while watching him from the corner of her eye.

He climbed in after her, then turned his head toward the door as he reached to close it.

Seizing the moment, she dove for her door. She had her fingers on the handle when he caught her— one hand digging into her shoulder, the other grabbing at her head. As he jerked her backward, her glasses went flying and her wig came off in his hand.

"What the..." he muttered.

A second later, he had her by both shoulders and was twisting her around to face him.

"Take that thing off," he snapped, staring at her head.

Numb with fear, she pulled off the nylon cap that had been securing her hair. As it fell free around her shoulders, Ben DeCarlo's eyes turned to icy blue steel.

He tossed her wig into the back seat, muttering, "Damn! I don't believe it. Of all the women in the world, I grabbed Monique LaRoquette. Witness for the prosecution."

BEN HEADED SOUTHWEST from New Orleans, along Highway 90 into the heart of bayou country, driving with one hand on the wheel and the other holding his Walther pointed at Monique LaRoquette. He still didn't know what the hell he was going to do with her, but he sure couldn't set her free.

What if I promise I won't run for a phone? she'd asked him back at the airport. *Would you let me go?*

Mentally shaking his head, he recalled that at the time he'd thought he might. Not right there at New Orleans International, of course. But he'd considered heading east from the airport and dropping her off in the middle of nowhere—then doubling back toward his destination.

It wouldn't have been the ideal solution, but there *was* no ideal solution. And at least it would have gotten her off his hands.

Now that he knew who she was, though, letting her go was out of the question.

She'd barely said a word since they'd gotten into the car, but she *had* admitted the only reason she'd come to New Orleans was to hear the verdict first-hand. Which told him just how much she despised him.

Of course, being convinced she'd seen him murder his parents gave her good reason to loathe him. But regardless of that, the fact she was convinced meant he'd be out of his mind to set her free. If he let her go, she'd do whatever she could to help the cops catch up with him. That *What if I promise I won't run for a phone?* line hadn't been worth the breath she'd used to say it.

Checking the odometer, he saw he'd driven almost fifty miles, which meant Houma wasn't much further. Once they'd switched cars, he'd feel a lot safer.

He glanced at Monique, who was staring straight ahead, tension positively radiating from her body.

"Turn on the radio," he told her. "Find some news."

Without looking at him, she pushed the on-off button.

"Still no trace of convicted murderer, Ben De-Carlo," an announcer was saying, "who escaped from the main courthouse at approximately 11:45 this morning. The police are presently combing the city in one of the biggest manhunts New Orleans has ever seen.

"Police Chief Royce Monk has asked for the public's cooperation and has announced a reward for information leading to DeCarlo's capture. A special hot line has been set up. Anyone with information about DeCarlo, or about the three accomplices who overpowered his guards, is asked to call 555-HUNT. That's 555-4868.

"DeCarlo is white, thirty-four years of age, six foot one, and weighs approximately one hundred and eighty pounds. He has blue eyes and sun-streaked brown hair. When he was led from the courtroom, he was wearing a dark gray suit, black shoes, a white shirt and gray tie.

"No one was injured during the daring escape, but Chief Monk has warned the public that DeCarlo is extremely dangerous and undoubtedly armed. Anyone spotting him should not approach him, but should call the police immediately. That hot-line number, again, is 555-HUNT.

"This has been a WKCK special update. We'll bring you more news on the story as it breaks."

"Turn it off," Ben said.

Monique reached over and pressed the button. "They don't even know I'm with you," she murmured.

"No. Everyone's watching for a man on his own." And the bulletin had said nothing about the cops widening their search beyond the city yet.

That had started him breathing a whole lot easier. As long as things went according to plan in Houma, he'd get clean away for sure.

"Nobody's going to be looking for me," Monique whispered. "It'll be days before anyone even realizes I'm missing."

When he glanced at her, her big brown eyes were luminous with tears.

"And...before anyone even thinks about trying to find me," she added, her voice catching, "you'll have killed me, won't you."

For a moment he was silent. Then he said, "Not unless you make me."

Looking back at the road, he realized his words had surprised him. Or maybe it was the fact they were true that was surprising.

Once, not that long ago, he'd *wanted* to kill her. After his first trial had ended, he used to sit in his cell wishing he could kill all five of the eyewitnesses who'd testified against him.

But he'd had two years to work through those feelings, and he'd gradually come to terms with the fact that the witnesses had honestly believed they were telling the truth. That they'd been certain it was him they'd seen in Augustine's.

So he no longer hated Monique. And at the moment, he actually felt sorry for her. She was clearly convinced he *was* going to kill her.

He glanced at her again, thinking that, terrified or not, she was a remarkably beautiful woman. Of course, he'd been aware of that all along—even back when he'd hated her guts, when she'd been on the stand testifying against him.

Monique LaRoquette was the sort of woman guys in Angola dreamed about. A perfectly oval face, creamy skin, high cheekbones and that long, reddish-golden hair.

The only thing wrong with her looks, to his mind at least, was that she was too thin. But he knew that went with being a model.

Not that she'd have been modeling lately, he reflected. She'd hardly have a high-profile job when she was in the witness protection program.

After a minute or two of trying not to think about how frightened she was, he looked across the car once more. "I'm really *not* going to hurt you, you know. Not as long as you do what I tell you."

She merely gazed at him, her expression saying she still didn't believe him.

That worried him. It might mean she'd have another try at getting away while they were stopped in Houma. Or maybe she'd cause a scene to draw attention to them.

Then what would he do? Shoot her? Turn himself into the murderer the world already believed he was?

Wishing to hell he'd never spotted her outside that courthouse, he decided he'd better try harder to convince her she was safe.

"Look…Monique, I didn't bring you along with the idea of killing you. I just needed to have a woman with me."

"And I was the lucky one you picked."

He swore under his breath. He could do without sarcasm when he'd only been trying to reassure her.

"Believe me," he muttered, "I'm not any happier that I picked you than you are. But I can't let you go right now. You already know too much."

"I don't know anything. I don't even—"

"You know I made it out of the city, that the cops are just wasting their time searching there. You know which direction I've been heading. So I'm not letting you go now. End of story. But that doesn't mean I'm going to hurt you."

Focusing on the road once more, he gave himself a swift mental kick in the butt. Snapping at her like that was hardly the way to convince her he wouldn't harm her.

They reached Houma and he drove across the Williams Avenue bridge, made his way to the street he wanted, then drove slowly down it until he spotted the black Bronco.

Seeing it gave him a distinct sense of relief. Once they'd ditched the Caprice, even if the cops somehow picked up his trail, they'd be searching for the wrong car.

Parking, he clipped the gun to his belt again and reached for Monique's hand. "Come on, we're changing cars."

When her gaze flickered to the world outside, he knew exactly what was going through her mind.

"Don't even think about it," he said. "Because I *will* kill you if you try anything stupid."

"I'VE NEVER RIDDEN in a Bronco before," Monique said once they'd left Houma behind. "It's a smoother ride than I'd have expected. Do you call it a van or a wagon, or what?" That was a pretty inane question, of course, but it was the only one she could think of.

When Ben glanced at her, obviously surprised, she tried to smile.

She couldn't quite manage it. Not while he was driving with his gun pointed in her direction. Still, she thought she *was* doing a reasonable job of concealing her fear now.

And that was a good start, because it didn't matter if she was shaking inside. Or that she hated him with all her heart. The important thing was convincing him that she really did believe he was going to set her free at some point.

If he thought that, he might gradually let down his guard. And if he let it down far enough, maybe she'd be able to escape.

"You can call it a four-by-four," he said at last. "Or some people call them trucks, even though they're not."

"Oh. Well, whatever, it's nice and...sporty."

That earned her another uncertain glance. He clearly hadn't expected chitchat.

But she'd been racking her brain for a plan, and the best one she'd come up with was to act civilly. And downright pleasant if she could handle it.

For some reason, she'd thought about the so-called Stockholm Syndrome—the one that caused hostages to develop positive feelings toward their kidnappers. And it had occurred to her there might be a similar syndrome that made kidnappers grow fond of their victims.

Ben was hardly likely to grow fond of her, though, if she was acting antagonistic.

Not that there was really much hope he'd start liking her even if she did her best to charm the socks off him. Not considering that she'd helped convict him of murder. But being sociable had to be worth a try.

"Exactly where are we?" she asked. "You said I knew which direction we've been going, but I really don't. I was too scared to notice anything at first."

Ben kept his eyes on the road, trying to decide whether he wanted to participate in Monique's game of Let's Be Friends.

She wasn't much of an actress, so it was obvious what she was up to, but he had to give her an A for guts. Here she was, trapped with a man she was certain was a cold-blooded killer, and she was trying to converse as if they were relaxing over mint juleps.

It would take more than a little friendly conversation, though, to make him forget that if he gave her the slightest opportunity to make a run for it, she would—and straight to the cops, too.

But what the hell. It probably wouldn't hurt to go along with her game.

After all, he was pretty safe now, so he no longer had to be on red alert every second. And since he was stuck with her, they might as well get along.

Finally looking at her, he said, "I guess there's no reason not to tell you where we are. We're southwest of New Orleans, in Terrebonne Parish, and if we kept going in the direction we're headed, we'd reach the Gulf of Mexico."

"We're not going that far, though?"

"No, we'll be stopping north of it. But we'll be in *serious* bayou country."

"Serious bayou country," she repeated. "You mean as in major swampland? Like Okefenokee in Georgia?"

He smiled a little at that—which made him realize he was *definitely* breathing a lot easier.

"There's not really any comparison," he told her. "I doubt Okefenokee's even forty miles across, whereas the entire gulf coast of Louisiana's lined with marshes and swampland."

"And the gulf coastline is how long?"

"Oh…the way it winds in and out, I guess twelve or thirteen hundred miles."

That news clearly upset her, but it was just as well. If she tried taking off on him after they reached their destination, she'd end up as some gator's dinner.

They drove without speaking for several miles,

then she said, "Ben? Now that you've escaped, what are you planning to do?"

"There's a cabin in the swamps that used to belong to an old hermit. Almost nobody knows about it, so we're going to hole up there." His answer silenced her for another few minutes.

"And after we've holed up for a bit?" she asked at last. "I mean, you aren't thinking we'll stay in the swamp for months and months, are you?"

"We'll stay for as long as it takes."

"What do you mean? Until they stop searching for you?"

"Something like that."

"And after they have?"

He took a deep breath, then looked at her once more. "After they have, I'm going to find out who *really* murdered my parents."

MONIQUE HAD BEEN SO LOST in thought she'd barely noticed when they ran out of pavement. Now, though, the Bronco was bouncing along a deserted dirt road she doubted had seen another vehicle in days.

This was the *serious* swampland Ben had promised. They were traveling alongside water, the shoreline thick with willows and huge cypresses draped with thick curtains of Spanish moss. And as they sped ever farther from civilization she was feeling frightened half to death all over again.

Who would have thought things could get worse than being abducted by a murderer? But the prospect of being held hostage in a swamp was the proverbial icing on the cake.

He was calling the shots, though, and if she didn't go along with what he wanted he'd kill her.

Doing her best to ignore the probability that he'd kill her, anyway, she turned her thoughts back to his last statement.

She knew she should have picked up on it long before this. But since he'd said he was going to find out who'd really murdered his parents, she hadn't uttered a word. And neither had he.

She had the feeling that he intended to outwait her even if it took forever, and it just might. She was too scared of saying the wrong thing to open her mouth.

All that reading she'd done about psychopaths had taught her a fair bit. She knew they were intelligent but totally without conscience. And that most were accomplished liars and could charm the birds out of the trees. Which explained, of course, why they so often got away with the things they did.

But despite what she *did* know about them, she'd never really been able to understand their way of thinking. And Ben was a concrete example of that.

He knew she'd *seen* him kill his mother and father. So why on earth was he bothering to pretend he was innocent?

Staring out at the swampland once more, she wished she hadn't begun thinking about psychopaths. Because now all she could think of was what would happen when Ben got her to some secluded cabin. And imagining what he had in mind was bringing her close to tears.

"Monique?" he said, finally breaking the silence.

"Yes?" When she looked uneasily over at him he

was watching her. Then he turned his gaze back to the road ahead.

"Yes?" she repeated after a moment.

"Look…I don't really expect you to believe I didn't kill my parents, but I didn't."

That made her wonder if he wanted her to tell him she *did* believe him. But that would be a ludicrous statement when she'd been an eyewitness.

"You've claimed that all along," she said at last.

"I claimed it because it was the truth. The killer looked enough like me that you all identified me in court. But I wasn't in Augustine's that day. And I've never killed *anyone,* let alone my parents."

She gazed at his chiseled profile for another minute, then looked away. That had been his defense, of course. The killer had supposedly been someone made up to look like him.

And he'd had an alibi of sorts, as well. His sister, Maria, had sworn he was having lunch with her, in her apartment, at the time the murders took place.

The media had called her a compelling witness. She'd even reduced some people in the courtroom to tears when she'd testified that she and Ben had been planning an anniversary party for their parents at the exact moment they were shot.

But the jury had chosen to believe the truth, not Maria.

"You followed the entire retrial, didn't you," Ben said.

Monique looked at him again.

"I mean, you were interested enough to be in that

courtroom for the verdict. So after you testified, you must have followed the rest of the trial in the news."

"I heard bits and pieces about it," she said, choosing her words carefully. It wouldn't be smart to admit that she really *had* followed it closely. She didn't want him asking her opinion about anything. Not when her answers might antagonize him.

"You heard about our star witness, Sandor Rossi, backing off from testifying?"

"I…yes, I remember hearing his name, but I really didn't catch the details."

"No? Well it was what Rossi told my lawyers that enabled them to get the retrial. He claimed he knew who was behind murdering my father and setting me up to take the fall."

When Ben glanced at her again, Monique nodded that she was listening—absently noting he'd said *father* rather than *parents*.

His defense had made a big point of the fact that Ben had been close to his mother. And that if he'd actually been the shooter, he'd certainly never have killed *her*.

Bethany DeCarlo, they'd claimed, had simply been in the wrong place at the wrong time. That was the only reason the man who'd been paid to kill Antonio, the man *made up* to look like Ben, had shot her as well.

"At any rate," Ben said, drawing Monique back to the moment, "Rossi provided enough facts that we were certain he *did* know the truth."

"Aah," she said slowly, thinking this conversation was truly bizarre. Ben had been found guilty twice.

Did he honestly think he was going to convince a witness for the prosecution that he was innocent?

He glanced at her, clearly expecting more than just an "aah."

She thought rapidly, deciding the smartest thing might be to go along with him, to sound as if maybe he *was* convincing her.

"Why," she asked, "didn't this Sandor Rossi testify at your first trial?"

"He said he'd just been too scared to come forward. But I'm sure that was only part of it. He probably got paid to keep his mouth shut."

"Then why did he come forward two years later?"

"Well, he told my lawyers it was because he knows my uncle—works for him off and on. And he knew my uncle figured this was an awful blow to the family name."

"Your Uncle Dominick?" she said, the question slipping out before she realized she shouldn't have asked.

Ben eyed her for a moment, making her extremely nervous. "How did you know his name?"

"I...I must have heard it in the news or something."

"During one of those stories," he muttered, "about the Dixie Mafia. About how my father was the head of a crime family, and how now my Uncle Dominick's in charge. As if that automatically meant I was part of it all."

That wasn't a topic she wanted to touch with the proverbial ten-foot pole, so she quickly said, "You didn't finish telling me about Sandor Rossi. The way you put it, that he *told your lawyers* he'd come forward because he knew your uncle, it didn't sound as if you think that's true."

"I don't. I think he only talked to my lawyers because somebody made it worth his while."

"You mean, someone paid him *again?* But this time it was to tell what he knew?"

"Uh-huh."

"Well who was it?"

Ben merely shrugged.

"But you *must* know who paid him off. If he was helping *you*, then you must…" She bit her tongue, realizing she was treading on dangerous ground again.

"Actually, I *don't* know. I asked my lawyers, but they said *nobody* had. That Rossi's conscience had just been bothering him."

"And is he a man with a conscience?"

"He's a man who'd rob his own mother for spare change."

"Aah," she murmured once more. So Sandor Rossi had only agreed to testify because someone had made it worth his while. Then he'd changed his mind.

But did that mean he'd taken the money with no real intention of testifying? Or that after he'd been paid off, a different someone had convinced him it wouldn't be wise to help Ben?

Looking out of the Bronco once again, she wondered who'd bribed Rossi to tell whatever he knew. Or who'd concocted a story for him to tell—which was far more likely what had happened.

Ben's uncle? That didn't seem very likely. From

what she'd heard, Dominick DeCarlo was convinced of Ben's guilt.

So maybe it was Ben's lawyers who'd trumped up a new defense. There'd certainly been *something* irregular going on with that defense team. It had been headed by the top criminal lawyer in New Orleans, the almost invincible Ezra Dean Slaughter. But part way through the trial he'd abruptly removed himself from the case—or had *been* removed by authorities. She wasn't quite clear on that point.

Of course, she couldn't rule out Ben as the one behind the sudden new evidence. Or it could even have been his sister. After all, Maria had gone out on a limb in court to help Ben—perjuring herself by swearing he'd been with her at the time of the murders. So it wasn't hard to believe she'd try bribery to get him a retrial.

For a moment, Monique wondered if she'd have gone to such lengths for *her* brother.

Not if he'd murdered their parents, she decided, a shiver running up her spine.

But maybe Maria honestly believed Ben was innocent. Maybe she'd convinced herself there *had* been a look-alike in Augustine's. That way, she wouldn't have to face the horrible truth.

Monique glanced at Ben once more, curious about the details of the story Sandor Rossi had backed off telling. She was leery of asking too many questions, but since Ben had been the one to raise the subject in the first place...

"Who," she finally asked, "did this Rossi say set you up?"

"He didn't. Not exactly. He just referred to the guy as The Nose—which he said was nothing more than his own code name for the guy. And I guess that's all it was, because my lawyers checked around and discovered The Nose didn't mean anything to anybody. At any rate, Rossi promised he'd name *real* names in court."

"He didn't, though."

"No. Somebody obviously got to him, because he sat there in the stand and claimed he didn't really know a thing. Even worse, he implied my lawyers had tried to put words in his mouth. That blew any chance of a not guilty verdict out of the water. That and Ezra Dean Slaughter taking a hike right in the middle of the proceedings."

When Ben said nothing more, Monique slowly sat back in her seat, suddenly aware she'd been leaning forward in interest. He'd sounded so sincere that if she hadn't known better he'd have drawn her right into his story.

She did know better, though. Psychopaths had a talent for sounding sincere, for making people believe them.

But even a top Hollywood makeup artist couldn't have made anyone else look enough like Ben DeCarlo to have fooled five people in Augustine's.

Then, just as she was thinking that, an image slowly drifted up from her subconscious. It was from earlier in the day. From the street in front of the courthouse. And it made the hairs on the back of her neck stand on end.

Chapter Three

Tuesday, February 4
2:52 p.m.

Monique sat staring across the Bronco at Ben, but it wasn't him she was seeing.

The image from earlier in the day grew stronger and stronger, until it became so vivid she was virtually reliving those moments in front of the courthouse.

She glanced along the street, looking for an empty cab, and her heart almost stopped when she saw Ben DeCarlo.

But it couldn't be. He'd been wearing a suit, not a sweatshirt and jeans.

Then, while she stood staring at him, looking for telltale differences, the real Ben had put his hand on her arm.

And that was when this nightmare had begun—driving all thoughts of anything else from her mind.

Now, though, she'd remembered about the other man, and the recollection was enough to make her tremble inside. He'd been standing about twenty feet from her. And from that distance she'd been certain he was Ben.

Her heart beating rapidly, she thought of how, in the courtroom, the defense table had been at least twenty feet from the witness stand. And it was from there that the eyewitnesses had pointed to Ben as the man they'd seen murder Antonio and Bethany De-Carlo.

In the restaurant, though, Ben had been closer than twenty feet to her. Hadn't he? But even if he had, the room had been so dim…

The image from in front of the courthouse dissolved into one of Augustine's. Then that horrible scene began replaying in her head for the millionth time.

She looked around when she heard a woman say, "Why, there's Ben," and saw an older couple sitting at a table in the corner.

While she watched, the man half rose and spoke. Then the woman started to say something more. But her words faded and her expression grew uncertain.

Why?

Until this moment, Monique had assumed Ben's apparent anger had caused his mother's reaction. Or that she'd spotted his gun.

But was it possible Bethany DeCarlo had looked puzzled because she'd realized the man she'd taken to be her son actually wasn't?

No! That *couldn't* be possible. Five people couldn't have made the same terrible mistake, couldn't have identified the wrong man and sent him to prison.

So what was the explanation for that man on the street today?

Monique realized she was digging her fingernails into her palms and consciously relaxed her hands, but it did nothing to relieve the tension in the rest of her body.

She *had* no explanation for that other man. No explanation unless she'd merely imagined him.

Which meant that had to be what had happened. After sitting in the courtroom, watching Ben when the verdict was read out…

She'd been so focused on him, and her emotions had been so intense, that when she'd gotten outside and seen someone who resembled him her imagination had simply run wild.

Yes, that would explain it. And it was certainly easier to believe than the possibility of Ben DeCarlo's look-alike defense having any solid foundation to it.

"We're here," he said.

She glanced at him, his words making her aware they'd stopped. Then she looked out and saw that while her mind had been miles away they'd left even the dirt road behind.

They were parked in a thicket of towering loose-limbed willows with water stretching out before them. Huge cypress trees stood rooted in it and lily pads clustered along the shore, while a broad expanse of algae covered much of the dark surface.

"Let's go," Ben said, opening his door. "We'll get our stuff out in a minute."

He didn't bother to grab her hand and drag her along with him this time, but why would he?

What was she going to do? Try to escape through the swamp in her high heels? With only the vaguest idea of where they were and no idea at all of how to get back to civilization?

Of course she wasn't. As much as she hated Ben DeCarlo, as frightened as she was of him, she'd have to stick to him like glue. Psychopathic murderer or not, she was totally dependent on him.

She climbed out of the Bronco, only then realizing they were parked on what looked like a wider than normal section of railway track without the rails.

When she stepped off the lengths of wood, she discovered their purpose. The ground was so soft and oozing with moisture that it seemed to almost bend beneath her feet.

"This way," Ben said.

She followed him toward the water's edge, the ground sucking her heels down with each step she took. As they neared the shoreline, he stopped and lifted one corner of a green-and-brown camouflage tarpaulin that she hadn't even noticed. It blended perfectly with the vegetation.

"I could use a hand here," he told her.

She helped him pull the tarp completely back, revealing a small motorboat. Then they got their things from the Bronco and loaded them into the boat—everything except her wig, which she left on the back seat. She'd hardly have use for a wig in the middle of a swamp.

Finally, they dragged the canvas over to the Bronco and covered it, making it disappear before their eyes.

By the time they'd shoved the boat into the water

and climbed in, she was wet up to her thighs and her suit looked as if she'd worn it every single day for the past five years.

Once Ben started the motor and they left the shoreline behind, Monique kicked off her sopping shoes and draped her coat across her legs for warmth. The damp chill in the air above the water was almost as cold as the chill of fear around her heart.

BEN HAD A GOOD SENSE of direction and more or less remembered the route from the times he'd visited the cabin. To be on the safe side, though, he kept checking his hand-drawn map, because the swamp was a confusing maze of open water, bayous, willow islands and channels.

That was why so many people—from eighteenth-century pirates to modern-day escaped cons like him—had used it to hide out. Getting lost was easy. Getting found wasn't.

And dammit, he'd really made it here! He almost couldn't believe that.

Of course, it was only step one. But being a free man after spending so long in that hellhole made him feel terrific.

"Ben?" Monique said.

He glanced at her.

"You *do* know where we're going, don't you?"

"Of course."

"You've been to this cabin before?"

"Uh-huh."

"A lot of times?"

"Enough. We're almost there."

"Whose is it? Now, I mean. You said it *used* to belong to an old hermit."

"Now it's mine," he lied, then looked away before she asked any more questions. Given the euphoric way he was feeling he might let something slip, so he had to be careful.

By this point, Monique would have realized how well organized his escape had been. And that he couldn't have orchestrated all the details from a jail cell.

Which meant she had to have figured out that he'd had help. But he didn't want her knowing, for sure, who it had come from.

The cops would be all over Maria and Dezi as it was—probably already were. On their list of suspects who might have helped Ben DeCarlo escape, his sister would be right at the top, and the manager of his wine bar—who also just happened to be his best buddy—would be number two. So telling Monique the old hermit had been Dezi's uncle, and that the cabin now belonged to Dezi, would be downright dumb.

A convicted murderer had nothing to lose, but Maria and Dezi did. When all this came to an end— whatever the end proved to be—Ben didn't want Monique LaRoquette being able to name names and point fingers.

They'd reached the inlet leading to the cabin, so he slowed the boat. There were snags he had to steer clear of. "It's just up this channel," he offered.

Monique glanced at Ben when he spoke, then sat staring across the front of the boat, watching for the cabin—and wondering if it was where she was going to die.

There was certainly no way she'd be able to escape from it on foot. She'd seen snakes in the water, and a few mostly submerged logs that she'd suspected were actually alligators. She would never risk trying to run away from Ben into the swamp. And even if she somehow got a chance to take the boat, she'd never be able to find her way back to real land.

Surreptitiously, she checked her watch once more. It had taken them less than an hour to drive from the airport to Houma, and barely half an hour from Houma to where they'd left the Bronco.

Adding the half-hour trip in the boat, that meant they were only about two hours from New Orleans. Yet, under the circumstances, it might as well be two million.

"There it is," Ben said. "On that willow island up ahead." When she spotted the cabin, a sinking feeling lodged in the pit of her stomach. The little structure was roughly constructed of weathered wood, with only one small window at the front. *Primitive* was the kindest word she could think of to describe it.

Reminding herself that trying to be pleasant was still the best ploy she'd thought of, she merely said, "It's built on poles."

He nodded. "Stilt houses are a good idea in a swamp. The floor stays dry when the water rises. And being off the ground usually keeps the alligators from coming inside."

She looked at him and thought she detected the trace of a grin. But as far as she was concerned, there was nothing even remotely humorous about any of this.

"'Course," he added, "a lot of snakes are good climbers, so it doesn't help much with them."

"Then it's just as well I'm not afraid of snakes, isn't it," she muttered. Given the situation, she wasn't finding it exactly easy to be pleasant.

Ben cut the motor and they drifted the rest of the way to the dilapidated dock. She eyed it warily while he tied up, deciding it was missing more boards than it had.

But they got out of the boat without incident and headed for the cabin. They'd just reached the steps when Ben stopped and looked down the channel the way they'd come.

"What?" she asked.

"I hear a boat," he said quietly, putting his sports bag on the steps.

When he tugged down his sweater, she realized he was making sure his gun was hidden. That started her heart pounding. As slim as the chance was, it might be a police boat coming. And she knew Ben wouldn't surrender without a fight.

Trying not to imagine what it would be like to get caught in the middle of a shooting match, she set her suitcase down beside Ben's bag and gazed along the channel—half hoping it was the police, half terrified it might be.

It wasn't. Their visitor proved to be a man in his early twenties who gave Monique a creepy-crawly feeling before he said a word.

Even though the afternoon had grown downright

chilly, he was wearing only a tight pair of jeans that clung suggestively low on his hips. A large knife in a scabbard hung from his belt.

Tanned and muscular, he had dirty, shoulder-length dark hair and a decidedly unfriendly expression. Clearly, he wasn't about to offer them a welcome-to-the-swamp drink from the open whiskey bottle dangling from his hand.

But that was just as well. There was no label on the bottle, and it was so dirty he must have been recycling it for months.

Cutting his motor, he drifted to the dock—standing with his feet spread wide for balance and appraising her and Ben through slits of eyes.

"Looking for someone?" Ben asked as the boat gently bumped to a stop.

"This ain't your place."

"It is at the moment. So is there anything I can do for you?"

"Name's *Duh-wayne*," he drawled. "But people jus' call me Spook."

Ben merely nodded.

"Jus' spotted you an' the lady a mile or so back," Spook went on, looking Monique over in a way that left no doubt what he'd like to do to her.

It almost made her squirm, but she forced herself not to move a muscle.

"Jus' wondered what you was doin' here."

"Uh-huh?" Ben said. "Well, we're just here to get away from the city for a while. Spend some time *on our own*," he added, his soft Southern accent more pronounced than usual. "So if there was nothing in particular you wanted…"

Spook took a swallow from his whiskey bottle, then began to slowly rub his thumb up and down the scabbard. "Jus' wanted ta see who ya' was. Jus' wanted…"

His words trailed off as Ben wheeled to one side, whipping his gun from beneath his sweater.

He stood pointing it in the direction of a stand of bamboo for a minute, then turned back toward Spook and casually tucked the gun away again.

"Sorry to interrupt you, Spook," he said. "But I thought I spotted a copperhead in that canebrake."

Spook glanced toward the bamboo, then looked suspiciously back at Ben. "Have ta be a durn good shot ta getta snake at that distance."

"He's an excellent shot," Monique said quietly.

Tuesday, February 4
5:29 p.m.

AS THE SUN SLOWLY dropped in the sky, Monique was getting colder on the cabin steps, even though she was wearing a cozy sweater and had her coat draped over her shoulders. But she wasn't quite ready to go inside.

Fortunately, knowing that if the deliberations had dragged on she'd be staying over in New Orleans, she'd packed jeans and a few other comfortable things to wear in her hotel room. She'd never imagined, though, she'd be staying in a cabin that was light years away from the Clarion Hotel.

A noise inside made her glance up at the door, which was standing partly open because Ben said he liked to listen to the sounds of the swamp. She suspected the real reason was so he'd know if she tried to make a run for it, but there was about as much chance of her doing that as flying.

Turning her gaze back toward the setting sun, she watched it grow ever lower, painting the sky a pale orange behind the stark shapes of dead cypresses. In a surreal way, the swamp was surprisingly beautiful. Beautiful but frightening.

And it wasn't only the snakes and alligators that had her feeling uneasy about it now. That bayou boy who'd come calling had scared the devil out of her. If she'd been alone, if Ben hadn't been with her...

She took a long, slow breath—remembering, again, how glad she'd felt that he'd been there to protect her.

The more she thought about that, the more it worried her. Did it mean she was losing perspective? That after less than a day the Stockholm Syndrome was kicking in? Making her have positive feelings toward her abductor?

No, she told herself. She wasn't having positive *feelings,* plural. She'd merely had a single, fleeting one. And only because, at that specific moment, Ben had seemed a whole lot saner and safer than Duhwayne-call-me-Spook.

But she wasn't forgetting that Ben DeCarlo was a psychopathic killer. Or thinking that just because he hadn't done her any real harm, thus far, she was guaranteed future safety. Even though he'd said he had no intention of killing her...

She realized she was actually starting to think he might not, and that took her aback.

Warning herself she was probably pushing wishful thinking to the extreme, she sat gazing out into the twilight for a little longer—serenaded by a chorus of frogs and listening to the quiet stirrings in the water and the occasional call of birds.

Once the sun finally slipped completely behind the vegetation of the swamp, leaving only an orange glow that was fading quickly to black, she rose and went into the cabin, pulling the door closed against the dampness of the night.

Inside, a fire was crackling in the woodstove, singeing the air with the smell of smoke, and its flames had driven the dampness from the room.

"Getting cold out?" Ben asked.

"A little."

He semi-smiled at her, which made her feel funny inside. It didn't seem appropriate for the kidnapper to smile at the kidnappee.

Then she found herself semi-smiling back, aware that being pleasant to him was no longer quite as difficult as it had been earlier.

After he turned toward the small kitchen counter again, and went back to cleaning the fish he'd caught from the dock, her gaze lingered on him.

He'd taken off the phony mustache, so he looked more like himself. But it was a different self than she'd seen before. During the trials, he'd always been impeccably dressed in designer suits. Wearing jeans and a sweatshirt, he looked more...

She forced her eyes from him when the words *ruggedly masculine* formed, then refused to leave her mind. But she couldn't help thinking he was an inordinately good-looking man—a perfect example of why you should never judge a book by its cover.

Carefully keeping her gaze from him, she surveyed the cabin, even though there was nothing more to survey than there'd been when they'd first arrived. And about the only things she hadn't noticed earlier were the oil lanterns that were now providing light.

One was sitting on the kitchen counter, another on the battered chest of drawers in the back corner. Her gaze drifted downward—to where a three-quarter-sized mattress was lying on the bare floor. It was made up with clean sheets and a blanket, and every time she looked at it she wondered what sleeping arrangements Ben had in mind.

She had a pretty good idea, of course. But dwelling on that only made her more anxious, so she focused on the living room area.

It consisted of a single piece of furniture, a couch someone had constructed from roughly hewn wood and broad leather strips. On the floor beside it, looking entirely out of place, sat a large radio.

"Battery operated, I assume?" she said, noticing that Ben was eyeing her.

"Shortwave."

"Oh, you can transmit from here?" If there was a link to the outside world and she could manage to—

"Uh-uh, you're thinking of *ham* radios," he said,

dashing her hopes. "I don't have a transmitter. The radio's just so I can keep track of what's happening."

Keep track of how the search for him was going, she knew he meant.

"Hungry?"

"Starving," she admitted.

"Sorry we had to miss lunch, but I didn't figure stopping to eat would be a good idea."

"No. Not when we were on the run like Bonnie and Clyde." The moment she said the words, she wanted to take them back. They made it sound as if she was on his side, which wasn't how she'd meant them at all.

But that was apparently how he'd interpreted them, because he smiled again—more easily this time. It started her feeling funnier yet.

"Well, these fish are ready for cooking," he said, dropping them into the sizzling pan. "So how about opening some wine? There are a couple of bottles in the cooler."

Wine in the cooler. Along with cartons of groceries on the counter. Someone had certainly stocked the cabin well.

And it had only been today, she discovered when she opened the metal cooler. The ice inside hadn't entirely melted.

She'd barely uncorked the wine before Ben was putting the fish onto plates—along with the salad he'd made.

Sitting down at the table with him, she couldn't help thinking how ludicrous the scene was. She was in the middle of the wilds, about to have a civilized dinner prepared by a murderer. It was akin to being dropped into the middle of a Fellini filming without being given a script.

Ben glanced at her expectantly as she took her first bite of fish, so she told him it was delicious—which was true. After that, they ate in silence. Then, just as he was suggesting they take the remaining wine over to the couch, he paused mid-sentence and looked at the door.

"What?" she said, her heart starting to hammer when he reached for his gun.

"There's someone out there," he whispered.

Chapter Four

Tuesday, February 4
6:51 p.m.

"Ben? It's me," a man quietly called from outside.

Monique watched Ben clip his gun back onto his belt. He didn't look as if he'd been expecting company, but at least this was someone he knew.

The door opened and the man strode inside, holding a suitcase in one hand and a rifle in the other. Mid-thirties, with dark eyes and hair, he was about Ben's height and weight.

"Thought I'd bring you this stuff myself, 'cuz..." He spotted her and stopped in his tracks, then shot Ben a silent question.

"Monique LaRoquette," Ben told him.

Dezi looked at her again. "Oh, jeez, it *is* her. I knew I'd seen her before," he added to Ben—as if she couldn't hear every word. "But why's she here?"

"Felicia didn't show. When I got to the front of the courthouse she wasn't there, but Monique was, so—"

"Okay, I've got the picture." Dezi waved off the rest of the explanation.

Ben nodded. Now they could get to what *he* wanted to know—which was what the hell his buddy was doing here. They'd been certain the cops would be watching Dezi's every move, so his coming to the cabin sure hadn't been part of the plan.

When he asked his question, Dezi's gaze flickered to Monique once more. Clearly, he didn't want to talk in front of her. But aside from sending her outside, Ben couldn't see any way around that, and he wasn't sending her out.

She had to realize she'd be crazy to try making a run for it, but she might figure getting lost in the swamp was the lesser of two evils. And the last thing he wanted was to be blamed for another death.

He gestured for Dezi to walk over to the window with him, which was as far away from her as they could get, then quietly said, "I wish she hadn't seen you. She'll ID you for sure."

"We'll worry about that when the time comes."

"Well, try not to let her know Maria was in on things, too, huh?"

"Sure. I'd already thought about that."

"So what's up? Weren't the cops all over you?"

"Yeah, they came to the Crescent asking their questions. And they had a couple of guys watching the place. But I ducked out the back and didn't use my own car. I was probably halfway here before they realized I was gone. And I've got an alibi for where I've been."

"Good," Ben said, feeling less uneasy. "But what

was with the sneaking-up routine? You're lucky I didn't take a shot at you.''

"Well, I spotted somebody down a channel a ways back. And I didn't want him following the sound of the motor, so I didn't use it much after that.''

"I think I know who he was. We had company earlier. Does the name Spook mean anything to you?''

Dezi swore under his breath, then said, "He's the closest neighbor. His cabin's a couple of miles from here. But I thought he was still gone.''

"Gone where?''

"Oh, once or twice a year he decides to head out of the swamp for a little excitement. And every time he does, he ends up locked away for a while. Either in a jail or a psycho ward. He doesn't exactly have both oars in the water.''

"Terrific,'' Ben muttered.

Dezi shrugged. "The good news is he'd never tell anyone you're here. He likes secrets.''

"He also seemed to like the knife he was wearing.''

"Yeah...well, just keep an eye out.''

Ben glanced toward Monique, who was still sitting at the table. Once he got to part two of the plan, and had to leave her here alone...

He forced that thought from his mind. It was another thing not to worry about until the time came. "So what's up?'' he asked, looking back at Dezi. "Why are you here?''

"I had to make sure you made it okay. Maria was goin' nuts and—''

"Why? What's happened?"

"You haven't had the radio on, have you."

"Not since we ditched the rental car."

"Then you haven't heard what happened to Felicia."

Ben's mouth went dry.

"She's dead. The cops found her in an alley. Stuffed into a Dumpster with her throat slit."

"When?" he asked, trying to ignore the sick feeling in his stomach.

"They found her while they were looking for you. Ironic, huh? But she'd been dead since sometime last night."

Ben turned to the window and gazed unseeingly into the darkness. It was happening again. Or *still* happening would be more accurate. Someone was still out to get him.

First, the guy Sandor Rossi called The Nose had arranged for Antonio DeCarlo's murder—framing Ben in the process. Then he'd convinced Rossi not to testify at the retrial. And now a woman had been killed so she couldn't help with Ben's escape.

But how had anyone known about the plan, let alone that Felicia was supposed to play a part in it?

When he voiced the questions, Dezi simply shook his head. Then he nodded toward Monique, saying, "What about her? What are you going to do with her?"

"I don't know. I should never have grabbed her in the first place. But when I was standing outside that courthouse with Felicia nowhere in sight, all I could think about was that we'd reserved the car in a woman's name. And that if things didn't go right at the airport I'd be screwed.''

"Okay, what's done's done. And we'll figure something out. When this is all over, we'll somehow convince her not to press charges."

"Yeah." Ben looked over at Monique once more, thinking the odds on them managing that had to be about as good as the odds on his finding the real killer.

10:17 p.m.

MONIQUE STOOD IN THE moonlight beside Ben, watching Dezi pole his boat away from the dock and wishing with all her heart that she could go with him—head back to civilization instead of being trapped here with a killer.

"Why isn't he using his motor?" she asked as the boat silently glided down the canal and disappeared into the darkness.

"He doesn't want to draw attention to us. Just in case anyone's within hearing range."

"You mean anyone like Spook."

Ben didn't reply, simply turned and started for the cabin.

Nervously, she trailed along. Given the choice between going back inside with him, or staying out here with the alligators and snakes—and possibly Spook— there really was no choice. But the prospect of going back inside had her very, very frightened.

It was bedtime. And even though Ben hadn't laid

a hand on her since they'd gotten here, she doubted that was going to continue for much longer.

He'd been arrested the day of the murders, over three years ago, and he'd been in custody ever since. So unless Angola was the type of prison that permitted conjugal visits—which she didn't think it was—he hadn't been with a woman in an awfully long time.

They reached the door and he opened it, ushering her in and surprising her by saying, "I'll wait out here for a couple of minutes—give you time to get ready for bed."

She hurried in and changed into her nightshirt and housecoat, unable to keep her eyes from straying to the mattress. Then, her heart in her throat, she simply stood waiting for Ben to come inside.

When he finally did, he said, "We'll have to share the mattress."

"I could use the couch," she tried, even though she knew he wouldn't go for it.

He shook his head. "There's only one set of bedding. And that couch is uncomfortable to sit on, let alone to try sleeping on. So just blow out the lantern on the dresser and take whichever side you want."

Ben wandered over to the kitchen area and stood surreptitiously watching Monique. Once she killed the light in the corner, she crawled onto the mattress without taking off her robe. Then she pulled the covers tightly up around her throat and lay there looking like a terrified rabbit, so near the edge of the mattress that half an inch more and she'd roll off onto the floor.

Blowing out the lantern on the kitchen counter, he

stripped down to his shorts in the darkness—resisting the impulse to tell her *he'd* try sleeping on the couch.

He'd thought his years in prison had buried any gentlemanly impulses so deep inside him they'd never surface, which made having one unexpected. But having it and acting on it were two different things.

You didn't really sleep in prison. Not when there were always lights on and the nights were full of voices—along with the intermittent clangings of steel and the occasional cries of some prisoner being forced to pleasure his cell mate. And after not having a real night's sleep in more than three years, he'd be damned if he'd miss the chance for one tonight.

Pushing the thoughts of prison from his mind, he crossed the cabin and crawled in beside Monique, careful not to get close enough to brush against her. He ended up close enough, though, that the intoxicating scent of her perfume began doing wicked things to his insides.

It took all of three seconds to realize he should have acted on that gentlemanly impulse—not for her sake, but his own.

Taking a slow, ragged breath, he told himself he wasn't moving to the couch. He was going to lie right where he was and control his urges.

Vicious animal, the press had frequently called him. That, and *psychopathic murderer* had been their favorite terms. But he wasn't an animal any more than he was a killer. And despite all the indignities of prison, he'd retained enough humanity that he'd never force himself on a woman. Regardless of what Monique believed, she was safe with him.

He lay on his side with his back to her, listening to her soft breathing, feeling her body heat…and aching to roll over and hold her.

Clenching his fists, he told himself it wasn't *her* he wanted to hold. His need might be almost overwhelming, but he wasn't desperate enough to want a woman who hated his guts.

It was simply that she was lying right next to him. And that she was beautiful. And that it had been so, so long.

He took another slow breath, reminding himself he wasn't an animal. Then he eased one hand to his face and wiped away the tears that had somehow found their way onto his cheeks.

Friday, February 7
6:43 a.m.

MONIQUE SAT ON THE cabin steps, hugging herself for warmth and gazing absently through the mist. She could just make out the first pink fingers of the rising sun—stretching upward past dead cypresses that were wet and dark against the pale gray of the morning.

A splash told her Ben had a strike, and she glanced along the shoreline to where he was standing with his rod. Dawn, he'd told her, was the best time for catching fish.

Watching him reel this one in, she let her thoughts drift back over the past few days, trying to decide exactly when she'd stopped being frightened of him. She wasn't sure. Just as she was no longer sure of so many things.

She reminded herself—yet again—about the Stockholm Syndrome, about the fact that it wasn't uncommon for hostages to develop positive feelings toward their captors.

But was that peculiar phenomenon responsible for her losing her fear of Ben? And for the fact that, incredible as it seemed, she was having to fight against actually liking him?

Or was it that the two of them had been together almost every second of the past three days. And in all that time, not a single thing he'd said or done would have led her to conclude he was either a psychopath or a murderer.

Don't forget, an imaginary voice whispered, *psychopaths are consummate actors.* She hadn't forgotten. Still, if she didn't know the truth…

Looking out over the water, she couldn't help wondering if she really *did* know it. There'd been a lot of time to think since they'd arrived at the cabin, and the more thinking she'd done the more doubts she'd developed.

What if, against all odds, Ben's look-alike story was true?

Somewhere along the way, she'd seriously begun to entertain that possibility, because she was finding it more and more difficult to conceive of him as a cold-blooded killer.

And that wasn't all. As hard as she'd tried, she just couldn't make herself believe she'd simply imagined that man in front of the courthouse the other day. The one who'd looked so much like Ben she'd thought it was him.

But she'd been mistaken. And since she had, how could she be sure she hadn't made a similar mistake when she'd identified Ben as the man she'd seen in Augustine's?

She glanced along the shoreline at him once more, telling herself he *had* to be guilty. *Five* eyewitnesses couldn't have misidentified the killer, which made the possibility he'd spent all that time in prison for murders he hadn't committed awfully remote.

Even so, it wouldn't stop gnawing away at her heart.

8:31 a.m.

STANDING BESIDE THE COUCH and staring intently down at the shortwave, Ben listened to the latest news update.

"Police Chief Royce Monk has just completed this morning's press briefing on the DeCarlo case," the newscaster said. "He announced that the Citizens for a Safe New Orleans group has matched the police department's reward offer for information leading to DeCarlo's capture. That doubles the reward amount to $100,000."

When Monique glanced up from the couch, Ben merely shrugged. But he didn't like that little bombshell.

Aside from Maria and Dezi, only one person knew where he was. Dezi had needed witnesses to his whereabouts on Tuesday morning, so he'd gotten his brother to come here and stock the cabin.

That made Ben more than a little uneasy. He barely

knew Louie. And even though Dezi swore Louie would never say a word, $100,000 was a lot of money.

"Chief Monk," the announcer was going on, "stated that despite the NOPD's extensive search of the city, and the numerous tips the force has received, there are still no solid leads to DeCarlo's whereabouts.

"The hot line is continuing to take calls, and anyone with information should contact the police at 555-HUNT. But the chief admitted that DeCarlo has likely left New Orleans."

Ben exhaled slowly. That was what he'd been waiting to hear.

"Police forces in all corners of the country are on the lookout for DeCarlo, and Chief Monk remains confident the convicted killer will be apprehended shortly.

"However, reporters questioned the chief about extradition proceedings, making it clear that many of them believe DeCarlo is basking on a beach in South America.

"In other news—"

Switching off the radio, Ben glanced at Monique. "I'm going back to New Orleans."

She looked up again. "You mean, today?"

"Uh-huh. I won't find the real killer by sitting around here. And now that they've decided I'm long gone, I should be safe."

He waited for her to say something about the prospect of being left on her own in the swamp. They hadn't discussed it, but they both knew that if he took her with him she'd try to get away and run for the cops. So there was no option but to leave her here.

Surprisingly, instead of saying a word about that, she said, "Ben, why try to do this yourself? Why not hire a private detective?"

"Don't you think I've done that? The minute the police arrested me, it was case closed as far as they were concerned. They weren't going to look for evidence to prove I wasn't guilty, so we went the private eye route. But after we'd tried three of the best in the city, we gave up."

"Because none of them found anything?"

"Not exactly. More because of the *reason* none of them found anything. They all backed away from the case practically before they took it on."

"Why?"

"Somebody got to them. Just like somebody got to Sandor Rossi."

"Do you really believe that?"

"You mean am I paranoid? By this stage of the game, I probably am. But yes, I really believe they were scared off. So do my lawyers."

"Scared off by whom?"

"By this guy Rossi calls The Nose. The guy who wanted my father dead and set me up. The guy whose real name Rossi was going to divulge in court—until he changed his mind."

"You're going to talk to Rossi, aren't you? Try to make him tell you who this Nose is."

"I'd love to, but he's disappeared."

"You mean he left town, or...?"

"I don't know. All Dezi found out is that Rossi

disappeared within hours of my escape. So he might have taken off, figuring I'd be looking for him. Or somebody might have left him floating in Lake Pontchartrain—so he wouldn't be able to tell me anything if I caught up with him.''

Monique was silent for a minute. "Who *are* you going to talk to, then?" she finally asked.

"I've got a few other possibilities."

"But...Ben, your picture's probably been on the front page of the *Times-Picayune* all week long. Do you think you can just wander around New Orleans without anyone spotting you?"

Eyeing her curiously, he told himself he was only imagining that she sounded worried about him. She might have been doing her best to hide the fact she hated him, but she couldn't possibly *not*.

"I...I was simply being realistic," she murmured, looking away.

"Well, you're not the only one who can disguise yourself. By the time I head out of here, my own parents wouldn't know..."

His words trailed off, his throat suddenly tight. Not two minutes ago, he'd said something about the murders. But every now and then, it would still momentarily slip his mind that his parents were both gone.

Clearing his throat, he latched onto the first topic he could think of to change the subject. "You know, in all these newscasts we've listened to, there's been no mention of a missing woman. By now, shouldn't someone have realized you've disappeared?"

She gave him a little shrug. "I didn't tell anyone I was going to New Orleans. And I doubt a missing woman from Hartford, Connecticut, would make the news here. But nobody will have missed me yet, anyway.''

When she didn't elaborate, he simply stood waiting for something more. She never really talked much about herself, but he'd discovered that she didn't like long silences.

''I told my office there was an emergency in my family,'' she explained at last. ''That I wasn't sure when I'd be back. I guess, eventually, someone *will* realize I've disappeared. By then, though...''

She looked away, but not before he saw her eyes had filled with tears. And that made him feel like two cents.

Being grabbed by a man she believed was a killer could only have been a nightmare. And even now that he was about to leave, she was probably still afraid he'd do something awful to her before he went.

But he'd never have known she was frightened from the way she'd been behaving. This was the first time since the very beginning that she'd gotten weepy.

Gazing down at her, the questions he hadn't been able to stop asking himself drifted into his mind once more. What would have happened if they'd met under different circumstances? If she didn't despise him?

She was a gutsy lady, and if things had been different she was the kind of woman he might have...

Mentally shaking his head, he told himself there was no point in even thinking along those lines. You couldn't change what was, and he had to play the hand he'd been dealt.

But if he had the choice, he'd at least turn back time and not do what he'd done to her. If he could relive Tuesday, he'd walk right by her outside that damn courthouse.

He watched her for another minute. She was staring at the floor. And even though she wasn't making any noise, the way she kept wiping at her eyes told him she was crying. Thinking back, he tried to figure out what had triggered it.

I guess, she'd said, *eventually, someone will realize I've disappeared.*

Was that it? The fact that she was so alone in the world she could vanish without anyone even knowing?

He ran his fingers through his hair, aware that until the last couple of days he'd never given any thought to what being in the witness protection program would be like. But it had to be damn tough.

She'd not only been convinced a killer would be seeking revenge against her, she'd been completely cut off from her real life. And he knew, only too well, how losing everything you'd always had made a person feel.

Hesitantly, he eased himself onto the couch beside her, the scent of her perfume reminding him of the longing he felt every night while he lay beside her.

Being so close to her in the darkness was the ultimate test of his willpower, and only his stubborn nature had kept him from sleeping on the couch or the floor after the first night.

It was just as well he was leaving. Because even though he'd been managing not to touch her, he seemed to be constantly thinking about how soft and warm she'd feel in his arms.

"Monique?" he said, trying to force the thoughts away.

She didn't even glance at him, just continued to sit with her head bent forward while he wondered if he'd do better to keep his mouth shut.

His sister was always telling him it helped to talk about things, but he wasn't at all sure that applied to him and Monique.

At last, deciding to risk it, he said, "Going into the witness protection program ruined your life, didn't it."

She looked at him then, her brown eyes dark with tears and her cheeks stained with them.

"And I guess you could never even talk to anyone about it, could you," he pressed when she said nothing.

"No," she murmured. "I...I said goodbye to my family. But since then..."

"Since then you've had to keep it all inside?" he offered quietly.

When she merely nodded, he sat watching her for another minute. "Do you want to talk about it now?" he finally asked.

She shook her head, but even as she did words began spilling out.

"I suddenly had nothing and no one," she murmured. "I had to give up modeling because I'd have been too easy to trace. And my parents... They're in Seattle, and I used to call them every Sunday. But after I... Some Sundays I'd have their number half dialed before I remembered. And my sister-in-law was pregnant, so she and my brother have a baby I've never seen. I don't even know if it's a boy or a girl. And my husband…"

"Husband?" Ben repeated. "I didn't realize you were married."

"I'm not, anymore."

"But…he wasn't with you? I mean, when you went into the program he didn't…?"

"No," she whispered. "He said he wasn't leaving New York. He's a stockbroker and he said…"

Ben simply stared at her as she wiped away fresh tears. She'd been married to some creep who'd cared more about his job than about her? From everything he'd seen, she deserved far better.

She sniffed a few times, then gave a miserable little shrug that made him want to wrap his arms around her and pull her close.

Quickly, he told himself she wouldn't appreciate being touched by a man she hated.

"The marriage was a mistake, anyway," she finally went on. "I was never really certain he was Mr. Right, and it turned out he wasn't. He had this thing about appearances, and I guess he only wanted me because he thought a wife who was a model would be some sort of trophy. But as soon as I had to go into the program, and wasn't going to be able to model anymore, I was no trophy."

"He sounds like a total jerk."

"Well…I should have realized how he was long before I did. But after that day in Augustine's I was very…*aware,* I guess is the word, of how uncertain life is. So when I got back to New York it somehow seemed that marrying him was the right thing. It was hardly one of my better decisions,'' she added with another little shrug.

"Everyone makes mistakes," Ben told her for lack of anything better to say. Then he pushed himself up from the couch and walked across the room. Because if he didn't put some distance between them, he knew he'd do something that would make her hate him even more.

Chapter Five

Friday, February 7
9:02 a.m.

Monique watched Ben put the final touches on his disguise, thinking that his trip into New Orleans wasn't going to be quite so risky, after all.

There'd been a terrific man's wig in that suitcase Dezi had brought—as well as a pair of horn-rimmed glasses. And Ben had done some tricks with the fake mustache and an eyebrow pencil that made his few days' growth of beard look more substantial than it actually was.

She gazed at him for another minute, wondering if she should even bother asking when she was certain his answer would be no. But if she didn't speak up...

"Ben?" she said at last. "I want to go with you."

He turned away from the mirror and looked at her. "You know I can't take you along. But you'll be fine here. I'll contact Dezi and he'll arrange for more supplies. And as soon as this is over, he'll get you out."

For a horrified moment, she couldn't utter a word.

"Ben?" she finally said, her voice breaking on his name. "Are you saying you're not coming back?"

"You thought I was?"

"Of course I thought you were! I thought you only meant you were going for the day!"

"Oh, that's why you didn't say anything sooner."

"But you've got to come back! You can't leave me here alone! What if that Spook shows up again and—"

"If he was going to come back, he'd have come by now."

"But—"

"I've been keeping an eye out, Monique, and there's been no sign of him."

Ordering herself to control her panic, she said, "Maybe he hasn't been around during the day, but a couple of times I woke up in the night with the feeling that somebody was outside the cabin."

Ben gave her a skeptical glance. "Why didn't you mention it when it happened?"

"I guess I just didn't want you to figure I was scared of the dark. But I *did* have the sense someone was out there. Haven't you ever woken up with a creepy-crawly feeling that somebody's been watching you?"

"Uh-huh, practically every night for the past three years. But I really don't think you need to worry about Spook."

"I—"

"Monique, I'm sorry if you're going to be nervous, but I'd be out of my mind to take you with me."

"Then just go for the day and come back. And I'm

not saying that *solely* for my own benefit. If you try to hide out in New Orleans, sooner or later somebody will—''

"That's the only way I can play it. Driving in and out every day would be more risky than staying there. And you just can't come with me. How could I try to find a killer and watch you at the same time?''

She took a deep breath, then said, "I know you're going to have trouble believing this, but you won't have to watch me. I won't try to escape and I won't try to call the police.''

He was shaking his head, so she switched to a different tack. "Come on, fair is fair. I *really* don't want to be here by myself. I didn't just make up that bit about Spook. I honestly think he's been spying on us. So if you'll take me along I swear I won't turn around and—''

"Monique, I can't trust you.''

"Yes, you can. I—''

"No, I can't. You think I'm a murderer, and I just can't believe you wouldn't be onto the police if you got the slightest chance.''

She hesitated, afraid to put her thoughts into words. If she let herself do that, it might make her believe they were the truth even more than she already did. But if they'd help convince him...

"I don't think you're a murderer," she said at last. "I mean...I'm not sure anymore.''

Ben stood staring at Monique, wanting to believe that so badly it hurt. Literally millions of people were convinced he was a cold-blooded killer, and it would feel so, so good to know someone like her wasn't certain. But he couldn't believe that any more than he could believe she wouldn't call the cops.

"I wasn't going to tell you this," she continued slowly, "and I know it's something else you might think I'm just making up. But I saw a man outside the courthouse on Tuesday. I was staring at him the very minute you came up to me. And he looked so much like you that I thought he *was* you."

She gazed steadily at Ben as she spoke, and hard as he tried he couldn't see a lie in those gorgeous brown eyes. She couldn't *really* believe he might be innocent, though. She'd just told him that to make him think he could trust her. And as for seeing a look-alike...

But what if she actually *had*?

"This guy looked *that* much like me?" he finally asked, unable to resist.

"Yes. And I keep thinking about him and wondering if..."

"If?"

"If *he*," she murmured, "might have been the real killer. Hanging around the courthouse so he'd hear the verdict as soon as everyone started coming out—like an arsonist staying to watch a fire he's set."

Even though Ben was still telling himself to be careful, that he couldn't risk believing Monique was being straight with him, his adrenaline was pumping like mad.

"And now that I've told you about him," she went on, "I might as well mention something else that's been bothering me."

"All right," he said slowly.

"During the first trial, your defense team kept saying that the physical evidence was a joke, remember? Talking about how the police never found the gun and that everything else was inconclusive."

"Or trumped up," he muttered. "Or tainted."

Monique nodded. "And they kept referring to all those studies that show eyewitness testimony is notoriously unreliable, and saying it was all the prosecution *really* had."

"But it was enough for the jury."

"Yes...mostly because of Brently Gleason, though. The media went on and on about what an impressive witness she was."

Ben stared at the floor, remembering her on the stand. Probably because she was an artist, she had an uncanny eye for detail. And she'd painted such an incredibly vivid verbal picture of the murders that listening to her had made him ill.

"So why didn't she testify at the retrial?" Monique asked.

He hesitated, tempted to tell her about that article in the *Times-Picayune*. But if he did she'd probably figure it was only a figment of his imagination.

"I'm not sure why she didn't testify" was all he finally said. "We just thanked our lucky stars she didn't. Not that it helped enough to change the end result. Sandor Rossi saw to that."

"Well, I asked, Ben. I asked Travis Shanahan, the prosecutor, why he wasn't calling Brently the second time around."

"And he said?"

"He didn't give me a straight answer. But after

seeing that man on the street, I can't help wondering if Brently started to doubt what she saw that day in Augustine's. *Who* she saw, I mean. And maybe that's why she didn't testify again.''

Ben exhaled slowly, trying to quiet the rapid beating of his heart. Monique sounded so damn sincere, but if he trusted her, if he took her to New Orleans with him...

"There was an article about Brently in the *Times-Picayune*," he said tentatively. "Back before the New Year."

"Yes?"

"Someone tried to kill her. It ended with a big shoot-out in the Aquarium, but there'd been a lot of weird stuff happening to her before that."

"What sort of stuff?"

"Well, for starters, her husband—who was an NOPD cop—disappeared just after my first trial, and everyone thought he was dead. But this article hinted that he might not be."

"And?"

"And he was with her in Augustine's the day of the murders. In fact, the article implied that her being there was a setup. That the husband knew about the shootings beforehand and was ensuring she'd be an eyewitness."

"So I was right," Monique murmured. "Brently didn't testify again because she knew she'd been manipulated. Which meant she could no longer be sure it was really you she saw."

Ben gazed at her, thinking she sounded as if she truly did have doubts about his guilt. And if she did, just maybe he *could* believe what she'd said about not double-crossing him.

He considered that, then firmly told himself that taking her with him would be far too dangerous.

What about Spook, though, with that knife of his? Spook, who Dezi had said was a nut bar. If the guy really had been hanging around…

But why would he have come lurking by at night when there'd been no sign of him during the day? Wasn't it far more likely that Monique had been imagining things?

Running his fingers through his hair, Ben told himself to stop worrying that he really might be putting her in jeopardy by leaving her here. Because he'd be risking his life by taking her along.

And not only that. If she *did* double-cross him, he'd also be throwing away the only shot he'd get at finding either the man who'd pulled the trigger on his parents or the mastermind behind their deaths.

Which meant he just couldn't gamble on trusting Monique.

FOR A LONG TIME after Ben disappeared down the channel and the sound of the boat motor had faded, Monique simply stood on the dock looking out at the swamp—wondering whether she'd have taken him along if their positions had been reversed.

Not likely, she decided. She probably wouldn't have believed him any more than he'd believed her.

But if he'd let her go with him, she really wouldn't have betrayed him. Not even if she'd had a hundred opportunities. Her doubts about his guilt had grown strong enough that she wouldn't have taken away his chance to find the real killer.

She reflected on that a moment, aware that the fact she was thinking in terms of a *real* killer—as opposed to Ben—meant her doubts about his guilt had gotten even stronger than she'd realized.

Maybe voicing them aloud had caused that, or maybe it had been something else. Whatever, she'd reached the stage of being practically convinced he was innocent.

Her thoughts drifted from that awareness to the fact she was on her own now. And try as she might, she couldn't ignore the sense of foreboding that had settled in around her. Despite what Ben had said, she was certain their bayou boy *had* been spying on them.

One of those times she'd wakened in the night, she'd thought the steps had creaked. The other, she'd been almost sure she'd seen a face at the window. Just for an instant, though, not for long enough to be positive.

She hugged herself, feeling a sudden chill. If she was right, it wouldn't take Spook long to realize she was alone. Or maybe he already knew.

Slowly, she let her gaze drift down the channel once more. The morning fog had burned off, and shafts of sunlight were making their way down through the growth in the swamp. There were a few birds roosting quietly in the trees and a couple of snowy white ibises hunting for frogs in the bullrushes.

And, as always, there were alligators—some camouflaged by the growth along the shore, others so fully submerged they were almost invisible until they moved. None of them had come near the cabin, though, so she wasn't as nervous about them as she'd been at first.

She was just telling herself everything seemed perfectly normal when a fish jumped in the tea-colored water, startling her so badly that *she* almost jumped. As the ripples spread out in lazy circles, she turned and hurried into the cabin.

She doubted the lock would keep a child out, let alone a determined man. But at least Ben had trusted her enough to load the rifle Dezi had brought and show her how to use it.

"I'll tell you what," he'd said. "If you promise not to shoot me on my way out, I won't leave you defenseless."

She walked across the cabin and picked it up, thinking it might have been a good idea to shoot a hole in the damn boat. Then they'd *both* be stuck here.

Instead, Ben was on his way to New Orleans— where he'd undoubtedly be killed on sight by the first cop who saw through his disguise. Or, if that didn't happen, someone was bound to turn him in for the reward money.

He'd avoided telling her exactly who he intended to talk to. But since Sandor Rossi had disappeared, she assumed he'd start with those detectives who'd backed away from his case.

And wouldn't all three of them rush to tell the cops he was in the city?

The distant sound of a motor brought that train of thought to an abrupt halt. The rifle still in her hands, she hurried to the window, praying it was Ben coming back.

When she saw it wasn't, her heart began to hammer. It was Spook making his way down the channel—his gaze fixed on the cabin.

Clutching the rifle tightly with both hands, she headed back to the dock. As she reached it, he cut his motor and drifted the rest of the way in.

"Well, that rifle don't look none too friendly," he said, his slow smile making her skin crawl.

"I'm not a very friendly person."

"No? Well, I saw your husband leavin'. So it seemed like a good time for you an' me ta get neighborly."

"Sorry, but I'm right in the middle of doing something. I don't have time for company."

"That so?"

"Yes, that's so."

Spook eyed her for a moment, then quickly swung himself onto the dock.

"I said I was busy," Monique told him, pressing her knees together so they wouldn't begin knocking.

Shrugging, he slowly started toward her.

She took a frightened backward step, then raised the rifle and tucked it against her shoulder the way Ben had shown her. Until a second ago, she hadn't been sure she could actually shoot anyone. Now she was.

"Get out of here," she ordered.

He stopped, but didn't back off. "Don't look like you know how to use that thing."

"Well I do. And I will if you don't get going."

When he shrugged again, she thought she'd won. Then, with lightning speed, he dove forward and grabbed the rifle barrel. She tried to hold on, but it took only a second for him to rip it from her hands and toss it into the water.

"Your husband kin dry it up later," he said, giving her another of his revolting smiles. "But we'll leave it outta the way for now."

Futile as it was, she turned and started to run.

He grabbed her by the hair and jerked her back against him. He smelled of whiskey and sweat, and when he snaked one arm around her waist she thought she was going to throw up.

And then, through her terror, she heard Ben say, "Let go of the lady or you're dead."

BEN STOOD ANXIOUSLY at the window while Monique threw her things into her suitcase.

Dezi had said Spook's place was a couple of miles away, and that didn't take long by boat. So in case the guy had any ideas about getting a gun and coming back, the faster they took off, the better.

Monique snapped the lid of the case shut and glanced across the cabin.

"What?" he asked. She obviously had something on her mind, but looked uncertain about speaking.

"I...I was still too scared when Spook left to say much, but you might have saved my life, you know. At the very least you kept him from..."

When she didn't finish the sentence, Ben said, "It's just a good thing I saw him lurking down that canal."

"It's an even better thing you doubled back and followed him."

After she said that, she smiled so warmly it felt as if someone had sucked all the breath from Ben's body.

"I guess what I'm trying to say is that I just don't know how to thank you."

"Don't double-cross me when we get to New Orleans," he told her, striding over and picking up her case. "That's all the thanks I want."

"I won't. I wouldn't have before, and now..."

"Now what?"

"When I first realized you were there, when I saw you in that boat with your gun aimed at Spook, I thought you were going to kill him."

"The idea certainly crossed my mind."

"But you didn't."

"No, I didn't."

He took a couple of steps toward the door; Monique remained where she was.

"Ben?" she said when he glanced back.

"What?"

"If you were really a murderer, you *would* have killed him, wouldn't you."

He gazed at her for a moment, afraid he was misinterpreting her words—merely taking them to mean what he wanted them to.

"I told you before," he said at last. "I've never killed anyone."

"I know," she murmured. "When you didn't shoot Spook, I knew for sure that killing isn't in you."

She didn't lower her gaze, merely stood watching

him. And there was no misinterpreting the invitation in her eyes.

It made him suddenly hot inside and drove every thought of Spook from his mind. Setting the suitcase on the floor, he stepped back toward her.

Wordlessly, she wrapped her arms around his waist and pressed herself close to him.

He merely held her for a minute, breathing in the freshness of her hair and the intoxicating scent of her perfume. He'd spent the last few nights lying next to her and aching to hold her. Now that he was, the soft warmth of her body against his felt so marvelous he could hardly believe he wasn't dreaming.

"I'm sorry, Ben," she whispered, gazing up at him.

"For what?" he murmured.

"For what you've gone through in the past three years. For testifying I saw you in Augustine's when it was someone else. For being so sure when I was so wrong."

"Shh." He buried his hands in the coppery richness of her hair and simply looked at her for a second, thinking how incredibly beautiful she was. Then he covered her mouth with his and kissed her.

She tasted every bit as wonderful as she looked and smelled—like rare wine and sweet fruit. And she kissed with all the passion of a woman in love.

That thought wrapped itself around his heart and wouldn't let go. But kissing him and loving him were two entirely different things.

He kissed her more deeply, barely able to think. A

woman like Monique would never fall in love with a killer.

But she'd decided he was innocent. So now...

His heart pounding in his ears, he broke their kiss before desire overwhelmed him.

"We've got to get going," he said, forcing himself to take a step backward. "In case Spook gets another bright idea."

Wordlessly, she reached for his hand. And hers felt so right in his it made his throat ache. Because unless he could manage to prove his innocence to the rest of the world, whatever had developed between them was doomed.

EVERY TIME BEN GLANCED across the Bronco at Monique he caught her watching him. And every time he did, she smiled.

It made him want to pull over and take her in his arms, but he couldn't do anything that might draw attention to them. He sure didn't want some state trooper pulling up on the shoulder behind them to see who was making out in the middle of Highway 90.

But once they got to the apartment... Hell, when he was aroused just driving along with her, what would he be like later?

"This apartment?" she said, making him wonder if she was a mind reader. "You're *sure* nobody will find us there?"

Us. She couldn't have any idea how hearing her say that made him feel.

"There's no reason anyone should," he told her.

"It was rented under a false name long before I escaped."

She was silent for a moment, then said, "Your escape was planned down to the last detail, wasn't it."

He looked over at her again, a tiny whisper of concern skittering through his mind. She already knew enough to put Dezi behind bars as an accomplice. And the thought of her learning about his sister's part in things...

"You can trust me, Ben," she murmured, making him almost *certain* she was into reading minds. "You still don't believe that?"

"There haven't been many people I could count on over the past few years." He *did* believe he could trust her, though. Believed it almost completely. But if he was wrong, he'd end up either dead or back in Angola.

"Well, you can count on me," she continued. "In fact..."

"In fact what?"

Monique hesitated. As hard as she was working at seeming cool, calm and collected, she was trembling inside. When Ben had come back and saved her from Spook... And then, when he'd kissed her...

She shut her eyes, trying to recapture the magic of that moment. Since the day she'd gone into the program, she'd felt as if her emotions were on hold. There'd been no one in her new life she could even be completely honest with, let alone anyone she deeply cared about.

Maybe that had something to do with what had happened back in the cabin. Maybe all those emotions that had been locked away for so long had been released, en masse, and focused on Ben.

But whatever the cause, when he'd kissed her he'd made her feel brand new—as if no man had ever held her in his arms before. And such a surge of longing had rushed through her that she'd wondered if he'd somehow reached inside her and turned on a switch.

It was the first time in so long she'd felt really alive. And really close to another person. So close that if anything happened to him...

Nothing could. Incredible as it seemed, she'd fallen for Ben DeCarlo. Faster and harder than she'd ever fallen for any other man. And she had to do whatever she could to ensure he didn't go back to prison.

"In fact what?" he asked again.

Taking a deep breath, she said, "I can help you."

For a moment, he was silent. She sat listening to the purr of the engine and the smooth hum of the wheels against the pavement, not exhaling until he quietly asked, "Help me with what?"

She looked at him and took another deep breath. "With finding your parents' killer."

Chapter Six

Ben stared out at the highway ahead, letting the implication of what Monique had said sink in, aware it had banished his last lingering doubt about her.

She'd already gotten what she wanted. Instead of leaving her in the swamp, he was taking her back to New Orleans. And by this point she had to know he'd never harm her.

So her only possible reason for offering to help was that she cared enough to want to—which meant more than he could put into words.

He couldn't let her get involved, though.

"Ben?" she said, clearly expecting him to say something about her offer.

When he glanced over at her a realization struck him, making him wonder why it hadn't occurred to him immediately. If he no longer doubted her, if he didn't have even a tiny, residual concern that she'd call the cops, there was no reason to keep her with him.

No reason except that the thought of being without her was enough to make his heart ache.

He let his willpower build, then forced himself to say, "A minute ago, you asked if I trust you."

"Yes?"

"Well, I do. So..." The rest of words refused to come out, but he knew he had to make them.

Regardless of how much he wanted her with him, it wouldn't be fair to her. It was too damn likely that things weren't going to work out the way he was praying they would. And if he and Monique spent any more time together...

"Look," he finally made himself continue, "I trust you enough that when we reach the city I'm letting you go."

He tried to keep his eyes off her after he finished speaking, but when she didn't say a word he couldn't hold out.

The moment he glanced at her, she said, "Ben, I trust you, too. And I know that everything I once believed about you was wrong. You never had anyone looking for me, did you. Never paid anyone to kill me."

"No, of course not. But this Nose creep did his best to make me look like scum. And that included threatening the prosecution's witnesses—using my name, of course."

She slowly shook her head. "Then I've been hiding out for more than two years when I never really needed to go into the program at all."

"Maybe you didn't at first. But it's just as well you

did. I mean, since my retrial was granted, somebody *did* murder those two other witnesses."

"To make people think *you* were behind more killings. Lord, whoever set you up played God with so many lives. Your parents. Yours. The witnesses he threatened and the ones he killed. That makes me the lucky one in this whole mess. I can at least go back to my real life now. With the retrial over, they have no reason to make you look any worse. But you..."

"Oh, Ben, it's got to happen for you, too. I wouldn't be able to live with myself knowing you were in jail because of me."

"You were only one of five."

"But the point is I made a horrible mistake, which doesn't exactly make me feel good about myself. And the only way I can think of changing that is to do whatever I can to help you."

"Monique, you—"

"No. I want my real life back, but I want you to have yours, too. And after I've been in hiding all this time, I can wait a few more days to let my family know it's over."

His throat tight, he looked ahead at the road again. He couldn't take her up on that. It just wouldn't be right. But dammit, he couldn't help wanting to.

"Ben?" she said. "I really *can* help. A woman was part of your original plan, remember? And the police are still looking for a man on his own."

"No. It would be too dangerous."

"Don't be silly. It would be *less* dangerous. If people see you as part of a couple, there'll be less chance anyone will realize who you are."

"I meant dangerous for *you*. If The Nose discovered you were helping me, he—"

"But he wouldn't."

"Uh-uh. It's just too risky, and I'm not only thinking about The Nose. Some of the people I'll have to contact aren't exactly up for any Citizen of the Year awards."

"Ben, I'm not saying I should be involved in everything, but the fewer people who know you're in the city, the better. So what about those private detectives? Why couldn't I go and see them instead of you?"

"Because they'd have no reason to tell you anything. I might be able to convince them, but—"

"I could *give* them a reason. I could say... How about that I'm an investigative reporter? That I work for a tabloid, and it would pay a small fortune for the name of whoever made them back off your case? If I guaranteed they'd remain anonymous as my source, it just might work."

Ben rubbed his jaw, wondering if it possibly could. "They probably followed the trials," he said at last. "They might recognize you and—"

"I've still got my wig and glasses. And even *you* didn't recognize me when I was wearing them."

She leaned closer and rested her hand on his thigh. It sent a hot surge of desire straight to his groin.

"I...I just don't know, Monique."

"Look, when we get to the apartment, why don't I call my office—tell them I'll have to be away a little longer. Then we'll simply see how things go and play it by ear, okay?

"Okay?" she repeated when he didn't answer.

He merely nodded, afraid of how ragged his voice would be if he spoke.

THEY GRABBED a surprisingly good lunch at a non-descript place on the outskirts of New Orleans—big sandwiches of salami and chopped olives that Ben called *muffaletas*. Then he phoned Dezi to say he was back, and asked him to pick up the Bronco from the apartment in an hour or two. After that, they made their way into the heart of the city.

It seemed to be overflowing with people, and when Monique mentioned the crowds, he nodded.

"This is the last weekend before Mardi Gras, remember? I'll bet there are 300,000 tourists in town."

While Monique was thinking that the bigger the crowds the less likelihood of anyone spotting him, Ben pulled to a stop in front of a drugstore, saying he wanted to pick up some hair dye so he could ditch the wig.

The way he was looking at her made her certain he intended to buy something else, as well. And that started her thoughts racing. In less than a week, she'd gone from hating Ben DeCarlo with all her heart to...

Loving him with all her heart, she silently admitted—even though the fact she'd fallen in love with a convicted murderer was awfully hard to accept.

But he'd been *wrongly* convicted. Whether the rest of the world believed that or not, she knew it was true.

Still, she couldn't quite hush the voice of reason that was telling her she shouldn't be staying with him.

That what she *should* do was get on the next plane to Hartford. Or to Seattle, so she could see her parents.

Yes, the only sane course of action was to get out before she got in even deeper. But her grandmother had always said that when love came in the door, common sense went out the window. And after all these years, Monique was finally realizing how very true that was. She simply *couldn't* leave. The mere idea of it made her hurt inside.

When she glanced over at the drugstore again, Ben was just coming out.

"We're almost there," he said, getting back into the Bronco. "Only a few more blocks."

Their destination proved to be an old apartment building on Royal, in the French Quarter. The building wasn't far from busy Canal Street—which marked the southwest edge of the Quarter—and its architecture was typically New Orleans. Built flush with the sidewalk, it was a three-story brick-and-stucco structure with ornamental cast-iron adorning the balconies.

Her hand tightly in Ben's, Monique followed him up the narrow stairway to the top floor. He unlocked the door of 304, and once they were safely inside he put down her suitcase and turned to her.

For a moment she merely gazed at him, her heart beating faster than a hummingbird's wings. Then she was in his arms, kissing him.

"Monique?" he murmured after a moment. "I didn't pick up any horrible diseases in prison, but if you think it would be a mistake for us to..."

She hesitated for a second, aware this was the final

chance to change her mind. Then her heart silenced that thought and she whispered, "No, I think it would be a mistake *not* to."

He gave her a slow smile, drew her close once more and kissed her again—turning her to jelly.

"There's a real bed in here," he said at last. "Not just a mattress on the floor." Taking her hand once more, he led her down the hall to the bedroom.

While she watched, he removed his wig and fake mustache. Then he closed the drapes against the sunlight, turned back to her and gently cradled the sides of her face with his hands.

"I want to tell you something," he said. "I want to be sure you know this isn't just about sex. That I've fallen in love with you."

"Oh, Ben, I've fallen in love with you, too." She wrapped her arms around him, feeling the threat of tears in her eyes. What if one of those unsavory people he'd be going to see turned him in? What if some trigger-happy cop spotted him and...

Pressing her cheek harder against his chest, she tried to force those thoughts away. Then his hands slipped to her breasts and his touch dissolved her thoughts into sensations.

Quickly, he undid the buttons on her shirt and slid it off.

"You are *so* beautiful," he murmured, undoing her bra and freeing her breasts from the lace.

When he stepped back and stripped off his sweatshirt and jeans, pausing only to take a condom from his pocket and toss it onto the bedside table, she gazed hungrily at his hard body.

She'd seen him wearing nothing but briefs before, of course. That was what he'd been sleeping in. But this was different, and his arousal was so apparent she could feel desire pooling between her legs.

She unsnapped her jeans and he eased them down, kissing her stomach as he did. His growth of beard was still new enough to be rough against her skin, but she barely noticed. Not when his kisses were making her feel as if she was about to melt away.

Finally, he skimmed down her panties, then his briefs. Drawing her onto the bed, he buried his hands in her hair and kissed her. His body, hot and strong against hers, made her ache with desire.

"God, Monique," he finally whispered, "I want to go slow and easy, but I don't think I can."

"Who said I cared about slow and easy?" she murmured, sliding her hand down to his erection.

He groaned at her touch, then quickly slipped on the condom and turned back to her, smoothing his fingers up her inner thigh, making her tremble.

When he reached the hot slickness and discovered how ready she was, he entered her—so big and hard it took her breath away.

Moving inside her, he quickly transformed the trembles into shudders. In mere seconds they began to consume her.

She held tightly to him, her breath ragged, as wave after wave of release washed through her. And when he came, she felt so happy she could almost pretend everything was right in their world.

His solid weight on her felt reassuring, and after he

shifted to his side and cuddled her to him, she wanted to stay right there forever.

They lay in the silence of spent embrace until Ben nuzzled her neck and murmured, "I wanted to kiss you all over. I wanted it to last forever."

She kissed his shoulder and tangled his chest hair around her finger. "There's no one to say we can't do it again. We've got all the time on earth."

But even as she said the words, she realized how silly they were. The truth was, they might have almost no time.

MONIQUE PROPPED HERSELF up in the bed and slowly trailed her fingers along Ben's jaw, letting her index finger come to rest on the sexy cleft in his chin—made invisible now by his growth of beard.

"What?" He gave her a lazy smile.

"I've been wondering why you don't look Italian. What self-respecting Italian has blue eyes? Or streaks of blond in his hair?" she added, brushing them smooth.

"The kind whose mother came from English and Scandinavian stock."

"But your sister looks Italian." Maria had been in the courtroom during the trials. And with her long black hair and dark good looks, she'd reminded Monique of Cher in *Moonstruck*.

"I guess my sister got all her appearance genes from our father," Ben said.

"Aah." She kissed his shoulder, wishing they could stay right where they were. But she could feel the pressure of time as if it were a physical presence.

Disguised or not, Ben wasn't going to be able to stay in New Orleans as a free man for long. Sooner or later, the police would catch up with him—and odds were it would be sooner rather than later.

"I should try phoning those detectives," she said.

"You're *sure* you want to do that?"

When she nodded, the smile he gave her made her feel warm all over.

"But if I get answering machines, is it safe to leave a number?"

"Uh-huh. There's a cellular sitting on the dresser. Even it the cops knew its number, they couldn't trace its location."

She watched as he rolled out of bed and walked naked across the room, feeling absolutely certain she'd made the right decision by staying with him. And certain that wild horses wouldn't be able to drag her away.

The police, though, an imaginary voice whispered, *would be a different story.*

Telling herself not to even think about that, she turned her attention back to Ben.

"There's only stuff for me in here," he said, digging a terry-cloth robe from the closet and tossing it over. "So I guess you should pick up a few things. As soon as—"

Monique froze. Somebody was opening the apartment door.

"The landlord?" she whispered as Ben dove for his jeans.

"Don't know."

"Wait!" she told him, scrambling out of bed and

tugging on the robe. "Stay right here. We don't want anyone to see you without your disguise."

He grabbed his gun from the chair and handed it to her. "Be careful. The safety's off."

Her heart began pounding even harder. Who did he think was out there?

Hiding the gun behind her back, she forced herself to walk out of the bedroom and down the hall. When she reached the living room, and could see into the kitchen, relief swept her. A woman was in there, standing with her back to the doorway and putting groceries into the fridge.

"Excuse me?"

The woman jumped a foot, then wheeled around.

Monique instantly recognized her as Ben's sister. "It's all right," she said. "I'm here with Ben."

Maria slowly walked out of the kitchen, her gaze taking in the robe, the bare feet, the disheveled hair. Her expression, when her eyes finally locked with Monique's, was one of pure hatred.

Monique uneasily brushed her hair back, then called, "Ben? It's okay. It's your sister."

"What are you doing here?" Maria demanded. "Dezi told me what happened. That you were at the cabin. But what are you doing here?"

Before Monique had time to explain, Ben strode into the room. He gave Maria a hug, then asked, "Was it safe for you to come here?"

She nodded. "One of us had to come by to pick up the Bronco, and Dezi got tied up right after you called."

"But you were careful?"

"Yes. They've stopped watching the house, though. They've decided you're a million miles from New Orleans. But...?" Her gaze flickered to Monique.

"We fell in love," Ben said simply.

"Are you crazy? The first chance she gets, she'll rat you out!"

"Ben?" Monique said. "Would you mind taking this? Holding it makes me nervous."

She produced the gun from behind her back and handed it to him—then looked at his sister. "I think having that gave me the chance to do whatever I wanted. And I know how hard this must be to believe, but I honestly have no intention of ratting Ben out. In fact, I'm going to try to help him."

"She's decided I'm innocent," he explained.

"And she's going to help you. First she testifies that you're a murderer and now she's going to help you? You *both* must be crazy."

"Hey," Ben said, grinning at her, "is that any way to talk to your favorite brother?"

"My *only* brother, you mean?"

Monique exhaled slowly. They'd obviously exchanged those lines a thousand times, and she could feel the tension easing.

Maria gazed at Ben with a look of grave concern, then slowly shook her head. "I hope you know what you're doing, big brother."

5:23 p.m.

MONIQUE WALKED OUT of Roger Tatavi's office building, hailed a cab and gave the driver Lloyd Granger's address. Then she sat praying she'd have more luck with Granger than she'd just had with Tatavi.

The detective had flat out denied he'd been pressured into dropping Ben's case, insisting he'd had *personal* reasons for bowing out.

So now she was down to only one possibility, because they'd discovered that the third detective Ben's lawyers had hired was dead.

Apparently of natural causes, but that was neither here nor there. The point was, Granger was her sole remaining hope.

But at least he was meeting with her right away. Even though she'd called late in the day, both detectives had agreed to see her. Telling them her newspaper was prepared to pay a good deal of money for very little information had worked wonders.

She glanced out at the street, almost wishing she'd let Ben come with her. She could use a little moral support. But the less time he spent outside the apartment, especially in daylight, the better.

As the taxi pulled up at the address Granger had given her, she smoothed the dark wig, adjusted her glasses, and reminded herself she was back to calling herself Anne Gault for the moment.

When she got up to Lloyd Granger's office, he proved to be a balding man in his late fifties. He had a stomach that hung over his belt, a firm handshake and a no-nonsense manner.

"So, Ms. Gault," he said, ushering her into a chair and sitting down behind his desk, "you said on the phone that you work for the *National Ear*."

She nodded. They'd decided that using a well-known tabloid, one people assumed had a lot of money to spend, would convince the detectives it was worth their while to see her.

"And just what do you want my help with?"

"Well, before I explain that, I want to make clear that you won't be identified as my source. I know the *Ear* doesn't have the best of reputations, but..."

Pausing, she took her checkbook from her purse and opened it to show him the checks were in the name of Anne Gault.

Fortunately, she didn't have her address printed on them, and she carefully kept her finger over the bank's Hartford address. She'd figure out a way of explaining that if she actually had to *write* a check. And, if she did, Granger had no way of knowing there were only a few hundred dollars in her account. But if he went for this, Ben would have what they needed deposited.

"Your name," she continued, "will never be connected with either the *Ear* or my story. I'll pay you with my personal check and make it out to cash."

"I see. And exactly what *is* your story?"

"It's about Ben DeCarlo. Between the retrial and his escape, there's a lot of national interest in him. And interest sells papers, so we're doing a story on him."

"Uh-huh? And where do I come in?"

Leaning forward in her chair, she said, "Mr. Granger, before DeCarlo's first trial, his attorneys retained you to look into some matters relating to the case."

The detective eyed her suspiciously for a moment,

then said, "I did a little work for them, but not much."

"No...no, you had to drop the case, didn't you."

"Yes."

"Well, all I need is the name of the person who convinced you to do that."

"I see."

She waited, her pulse racing. He was at least considering the proposition, which was more than Roger Tatavi had done.

"And if such a person existed," he said at last, "how much would the name be worth to you?"

"Twenty thousand," she told him, hoping it was enough to make him bite. They'd decided that offering anything more might sound too suspicious.

"Do you have a card, Ms. Gault? I'll have to give this some thought."

"I...of course." She opened her purse, and started digging through it, swearing to herself. Now what did she do? The only cards she had identified her as a Hartford, Connecticut, real estate agent.

"Oh, Lord," she finally said. "I just changed purses, and I must have left my card case in the other one. But let me give you my number."

She scribbled the cell phone's number onto a piece of paper and passed that across the desk to him. "You'll definitely call me? One way or the other?"

"I'll definitely call you."

Sticking the checkbook back into her purse, she rose to go.

"One other thing," he said, coming around his desk to see her out.

"Yes?"

"How flexible is your paper about that twenty thousand?"

Her heart skipped a beat. "If we had to, I think we might be able to come up with a little more."

He opened the door. "I'll be in touch, Ms. Gault."

Chapter Seven

Ben paced across the living room once more, restless as a caged tiger.

If he'd gone along with Monique and waited out on the street while she'd talked to those two detectives, he'd already know how things had gone.

She'd been right, though. Every time he left the apartment he'd be taking a risk, and one bit of bad luck could end him up back in Angola. Or dead.

But he hated the idea that other people were doing more to help him than he was able to do himself. First Maria and Dezi, and now Monique.

Stopping at the window, he gazed out into the darkness, aware that the fact Monique *was* helping him still hadn't fully sunk in. Her falling in love with him was the most unlikely, improbable…

Hell, it was every bit as unlikely and improbable as his falling in love with her.

He smiled to himself, thinking how terrific she was and how great just being with her made him feel. If only there was a better chance that things would work out right, that he could be with her forever, he wouldn't still be so worried that letting her stay with him had been a major mistake.

On the street below, a taxi pulled to a stop. And when he saw it was her getting out, relief washed over him. He'd been telling himself she'd be perfectly safe, but seeing she actually was made him realize just how anxious he'd been.

Watching her make her way past a group of Carnival celebrators, his pulse began to race. In another minute or two, he'd know if she'd gotten the name he so desperately needed.

Not that he expected The Nose had leaned on those detectives personally. He'd have had someone else do his dirty work. But if Monique had learned who that someone was, it would be a good starting place.

Ben strode over to the door, and as the sound of her footsteps neared the apartment he checked the peephole to make sure nobody else was in sight. Then he opened the door—doing his best not to appear overly expectant.

Apparently, his best wasn't very good, because she took one look at him and said, "I don't know yet. Roger Tatavi was a complete waste of time," she added, shutting the door. "But Lloyd Granger is thinking it over."

Ben wrapped his arms around her and held her close, telling himself that thinking it over was a hell of a lot better than nothing.

"Then he admitted *someone* convinced him to drop

my case?'' he asked, letting her go so she could take off her coat.

"No, he didn't admit a thing. But he was interested in how high the *Ear* would go if, as he put it, such a person existed. And he promised to call me, one way or another.''

"Did he say when?''

"No.''

She stood eying him. "What?'' he asked.

"You dyed your hair while I was gone.''

"And it makes me look different enough?''

"Yes,'' she said slowly. "It's a lot darker. And if I trim it for you—change the style—I think it'll be as good as the wig. I miss the blond streaks, though,'' she added, reaching to touch where they'd been.

Catching her hand in his, he drew her close to kiss her. But just as he was about to the cell phone started ringing and they both froze.

Then he glanced at it, sitting on the coffee table. "It could be Dezi,'' he said, looking at Monique again. "Or Maria.''

"Or Granger.''

"Right. So you'd better answer it.''

Her heart in her throat, Monique hurried over to the table and grabbed the phone. "Anne Gault,'' she said.

"Lloyd Granger, Ms. Gault.''

She nodded to Ben. "Yes, Mr. Granger. Thanks for calling so quickly.''

He grunted an acknowledgment of that, then said, "Don't get your hopes up, because we haven't got a deal.''

Her heart sank.

"But I'm going to give you a little free advice, in case you don't know what a dangerous game you're playing."

"Pardon me?"

"The *National Ear*'s never heard of you. And they haven't got a story on Ben DeCarlo in the works."

Frantically, she tried to think of a way to save the situation. With the *Ear* publishing in Florida, they'd figured they'd be safe—that between the hour's time difference and going into a weekend, nobody would be in the tabloid's offices. But what did she say now that Granger was on to her?

"Did you actually think I wouldn't check?" he was continuing. "When I'm a detective?"

"I...I'm sorry," she said, still thinking furiously. "I'm actually writing the DeCarlo article on spec, just hoping to sell it. But I didn't think you'd agree to see me if I said that."

"Yeah? And a freelance writer has twenty thousand bucks to pay for a name? You think I was born yesterday?"

"I—"

"Look, I know you're not writing any damn article. And I've got a pretty good idea what you *are* doing. But like I said, you'd better keep in mind you're playing a dangerous game. New Orleans is a rough town. And if you ask the wrong person the wrong question, you'll end up in the Mississippi—wearing cement shoes."

Granger clicked off in her ear.

She put down the phone, blinking back tears.

"No go?" Ben said quietly.

She shook her head. "He checked with the *Ear.*"

"Dammit. How did he get hold of anybody?"

"Well, as he pointed out, he *is* a detective." One of her tears escaped and she wiped it away.

A second later, Ben was beside her. "It's okay," he whispered, drawing her into his arms. "You did your best. We'll just have to try a different angle."

"But now we'll be into those people who aren't up for Citizen of the Year awards," she said against his chest.

"Not necessarily. I've got one other possibility who's not pond scum. His name's Farris Quinn, and he's a reporter with the *Times-Picayune.* He might be willing to help me out."

Or, Monique couldn't keep from thinking, *he might call the cops on you.*

FARRIS QUINN WASN'T AT the newspaper offices, but whoever answered the line was happy to give Ben his cellular number.

"Okay," he said, glancing along the couch at Monique before he punched the number in. "We know what we want him to do, and there's no way he'll realize I'm right here in New Orleans. So we're not missing anything this time, are we?"

He waited while she thought things through once more. After it had taken Lloyd Granger all of half an hour to learn there was no Anne Gault with the *Ear,* neither of them wanted another screwup.

"You're absolutely positive nobody can trace that cellular number?"

"If anyone managed to, they'd find it belongs to a woman who doesn't exist and that the bills go to a post office box number."

"Then I think we should be okay," she said slowly. "But, you know, you haven't told me *why* you figure this Quinn might be willing to help."

"Because he's the one who wrote that article I told you about."

"The one about someone trying to kill Brently Gleason?"

"Right. So he's got to be convinced this whole case is fishy enough to make bouillabaisse out of. Plus, right after my parents were murdered, when all the other reporters were calling for my head on a plate, Quinn wrote a few pieces that were downright rational."

"Saying?"

"Well, he pointed out that I was an intelligent man with no history of insanity or drug abuse. And he asked a lot of obvious questions nobody else bothered to—including the cops. The same sort of questions my defense team asked during my trials. Why would a man like me kill his parents at all, let alone in Augustine's at high noon? And why would I kill my mother, when it was only my father I'd been having conflict with?"

"I asked those questions myself," Monique said. "Even back when I was certain you were guilty as sin. But you seemed *so* angry in that restaurant.

"Sorry," she added quickly, "that was just a slip of the tongue. I meant, *he* seemed so angry."

"It's okay." It was a slip that had made his bones go cold, though.

"He seemed so angry," she went on, "it wasn't hard to believe he was a man who'd lost all perspective."

"And, of course, he knew exactly what to say. To make people think he was me, I mean."

The words, Ben was certain, would be etched in his brain forever. At the time, the papers had printed them over and over again. Then the witnesses had repeated them in court.

I won't run for the Senate, the killer had told Antonio DeCarlo. *I'm sick of you interfering in my life. You may run this town, but you don't run me!*

"Ben? *Who* would have known just what to say? Could there be a clue in that?"

"No, I don't think so. My father and I had been having that argument for a while, and it was pretty common knowledge he wanted me to go into politics."

"Why did he?"

"Well, you know what *business* he was in. And people like him sometimes need political favors. So he decided that since I'd refused to follow in his footsteps, I should get elected to a position where I could at least help him out from time to time."

"Really?"

"Yes, really. You have no idea what those people are like, Monique."

"And why aren't you? I mean, I'm very glad you're not, but growing up under your father's influence..."

"I don't know why. Maybe it was my mother, but for some reason I developed a decent sense of right and wrong. And after I realized what my father was, back when I was just a kid, it changed everything between us.

"I...*hated* is too strong a word, but I never felt close to him after that. I always wished he was a bricklayer or a teacher or anything except part of the Dixie Mafia. But never, in a million years, would I have killed him."

"I know," Monique said softly. "So let's get on with proving that."

Ben draped his arm over her shoulder and gave her a long, lingering kiss, wishing he could spend the rest of the evening doing nothing but kissing her. Then he reluctantly reached for the phone and called Farris Quinn.

"Quinn," the man answered in a harried voice.

"Do you have a few minutes?"

"Who is this?"

"Ben DeCarlo."

There was a silence, then Quinn said, "How do I know that? Tell me something that wasn't in the news."

"Do you have a pencil handy?"

"Uh-huh."

"Okay, take down this number—555-1623. It's my sister's unlisted line. Call and say I told you to ask how she got the scar on her right thigh. When she was a kid, she tripped carrying a big pair of scissors."

"How do I know I'll really be talking to her?"

"Go pay her a visit if you'd rather."

"I'll start with a phone call. So give me *your* number and I'll get back to you once I've talked to her."

"Uh-uh. We'll talk first, and then you can check me out with her. I'm not in the country, and there's no point in running up your long distance bill."

The reporter gave a short bark of a laugh, then muttered, "Real thoughtful of you."

"You know I can't let *anyone* find out where I am, Quinn. But I need help. I want to prove I'm innocent, and that's a pretty tall order when I don't dare come anywhere within a thousand miles of New Orleans."

"And you want *me* to help you?"

"Yes. You cover a lot of crime stories. Which means you know a lot of cops."

"Some."

"Well, a woman named Felicia Williams was murdered the night before I escaped. The cops found her body in an alley, and I need to find out whatever they know about that killing. Suspects, any evidence, whatever there is." *Anything*, he silently added, *that might lead me to her killer.*

"She had something to do with your escape?"

"No." Which wasn't *exactly* a lie. Maybe she was *supposed* to have helped with it, but she hadn't been there outside the courthouse to meet him.

"So why do you want to know about her murder?"

"I can't tell you that right now."

"Then why should I go poking around for you?"

"Because I'm hot news. And if I can track down the man who actually killed my parents, you'll get an exclusive from me."

"And if you can't?"

"I'll still give you a story. You've got my word on it. And if anything happens to me," he added, glancing at Monique, "there's somebody else who'll tell you everything I could have."

"Who?"

"A friend in New Orleans. Her name is Anne, and I'm going to give you her number," he added, rattling off the cell phone number. "You can get a message to me, through her, after you find out about Felicia."

Ben waited a moment, and when the reporter didn't reply, he said, "I'm really not guilty, Quinn. If you help me, you'll be helping find the true killer."

There was another silence, then Quinn said, "I'll see what I can do."

Putting down the phone, Ben reached for Monique's hand. "He went for it."

"Oh, Ben," she whispered, giving him a hard hug. Then she drew back a little, her arms still loosely around his neck, and said, "I started wondering about something while I was listening."

"Uh-huh?"

"When you first told me about this idea, you said The Nose had to be behind Felicia's murder. That he'd somehow heard about your escape plan and was trying to thwart it."

Ben nodded.

"Well, why wouldn't he have just called the police and told them you were going to try an escape? They'd have had every cop in the city surrounding that courthouse."

"You're right, they would. But I told you earlier,

you have no idea what people like The Nose are like. You don't think the way they do.

"See, whoever he is, the cops are his enemies. So he'd never give them the satisfaction of gunning me down in the street. He wanted to take care of things his own way."

"But his plan didn't work. You got away without Felicia's help, so he had her killed for nothing."

"And, trust me, he thought absolutely nothing of doing it. As for his plan, maybe he had some backup that failed or... I don't know, Monique. All I know is that he's someone who hated my father enough to kill him. And hated me enough to frame me."

"How many people like that can there be?"

He shrugged. "A lot of people hated my father. But I have no idea who'd hate me that much."

ACCORDING TO BEN, during the last couple of weeks before Fat Tuesday there were parades in various parts of New Orleans every day and night. One of the biggest was on Canal Street that evening, and he'd said there was no point in going out until it was over and the crowds dispersed a little.

After dinner, standing out on the balcony with him and looking along Royal to Canal, Monique saw what he meant. The French Quarter was wall-to-wall people, and thousands of spectators had been lined up on Canal long before the first glittering float passed—the one carrying the parade's king, costumed like Henry VIII.

It was followed by an endless stream of others, many lit by torches, all bearing elaborately costumed people. Between the floats, marching bands strutted their stuff, while police on motorcycles and horses tried to keep some semblance of order.

The parade was as noisy as it was colorful, and when there were breaks in the music the air was filled with the sound of onlookers screaming, "Throw me something, mister!"—prompting the maskers on the floats to toss strings of plastic beads and other favors.

"This city," Ben said, wrapping his arm around Monique's waist, "goes so crazy for two weeks each year that a lot of Orleanians can't stand it. So they spend Carnival skiing in Colorado and call themselves the Krewe of Aspen."

"Krewe?"

"It's what the societies that sponsor the parades are called."

She nodded, then looked toward Canal again—realizing she'd been so caught up in the excitement that she'd momentarily stopped thinking about their plans for later.

But the prospect of paying a visit to Sandor Rossi's apartment was front and center in her mind once more. And it made her more than a little nervous, even though she knew it was the next logical move.

They had to learn who'd made him decide not to testify. If they could do that, they'd have The Nose's identity. Or at least the identity of one of his top men. But to find out what they wanted, they had to find Rossi, so Ben figured they should check his place for clues about where he'd gone.

Of course, as they'd speculated earlier, Rossi might be floating in Lake Pontchartrain. And that thought made her stomach queasy. Lloyd Granger had warned her she was playing a dangerous game. He could well have added that it was one she had no experience at.

"The parade has to be almost done," Ben said, turning away from the railing. "So I'll go give Dezi a call and make sure there's still been no sign of Rossi."

"Wouldn't Dezi have called *you*, if there had been?"

"Yeah…I guess you're right. Which means we might as well just head over to the apartment and see what we can find."

He stood eying her for a moment, finally taking her hands and drawing her into his arms. "It'll be safe," he said against her hair. "The cops really do think I'm a million miles away. They've stopped watching Maria, and Dezi's certain they're not hanging around the wine bar anymore, either. So there's no way they'll be staking out Rossi's apartment."

"But how do we get in?"

"With this." Ben produced a key from his pocket. "Somebody borrowed the super's master key for long enough to make a copy."

"*Somebody?*"

"A friend of a friend."

A friend of either Dezi or Maria, she knew he meant, but it didn't matter where the key had come from. What mattered was that at least they wouldn't have to stand out in the hallway trying to open Rossi's door with a credit card or nail file.

She went into the bedroom to put her Cleopatra wig and glasses on again, and when she came back out

Ben was on the balcony once more, gazing down onto the street.

"It's going to be bumper-to-bumper traffic for a while yet," he told her. "We'll make better time by walking a few blocks before we catch a cab."

Grabbing their coats, they headed down to the street, fears tumbling all over one another in Monique's mind.

This was the first time Ben had been out of the apartment since they'd arrived—the first *real* test of his disguise. What if it wasn't as good as they thought and someone recognized him? Or what if the police *did* have Rossi's apartment staked out? Or what if...

She swallowed hard. What if Rossi hadn't skipped town and wasn't floating in Lake Pontchartrain, either? What if they walked into his apartment and found his dead body?

10:43 p.m.

SANDOR ROSSI LIVED in a low-rise building up near Bayou St. John, which according to Ben was the only remaining bayou in New Orleans.

When the copied master key worked at the entrance, Monique's rapid pulse began to slow a little. And when they passed no one on their way to Rossi's apartment, it dropped almost back to normal.

Ben unlocked the door and turned on the light, revealing a neat living room without, to her vast relief, a corpse on the floor. But this wasn't the only room.

"Why don't you have a look around in here," Ben suggested, "while I try the bedroom."

She nodded, wondering if the possibility there was a body in it had occurred to him, too. She didn't ask, though, and when all was quiet after he'd gone into it, she knew they were okay in that department.

There was nothing sitting on the couch, chair or television set, and nothing on the coffee table but a TV guide, a remote and a couple of unpaid bills. The end table held a stack of magazines—*Penthouse, Playboy* and *Soldier of Fortune*. But no clues.

Wandering into the kitchen, she glanced over at the phone on the counter. Beside it were a message pad and small address-phone number book—lying open.

Her fingertips tingling with excitement, she quickly crossed to the counter. The pad was blank, so she turned her attention to the book. It was open at the *G* page, and there were half a dozen names on it. Some had addresses noted, some only phone numbers.

One of these people was likely the last person Rossi called before he disappeared. But which one?

She started playing eenie-meenie with the names, then remembered something she'd once seen in a movie. Grabbing a pencil from beside the message pad, she picked up the receiver and pressed the redial button, listening carefully as the phone dialed. Once she'd jotted down the numbers, she slowly lowered the receiver and searched to see if the phone number corresponded with any on the page he'd left open.

It did. The name written beside the number was simply Grace. But the fact he'd called some woman didn't necessarily mean that—

"Monique?" Ben said.

When she turned, he was standing in the kitchen doorway, his eyes alive with excitement.

"I know where he went. Look what I found in the bedroom garbage."

He handed her a crumpled piece of paper. There was a flight number written on it, and the words, *Arrives La Guardia at 7:17.*

Her heart skipped a beat and she gestured toward the book. "Ben, the last person he phoned was whoever that Grace is. And I lived in Manhattan long enough to know that the area code 718 means she lives somewhere in the boroughs. But that's an awfully big somewhere."

Ben stared at the page for a minute, then said, "Why is she under *G* for Grace, when everyone else is listed by surname?"

"Because she's someone he knows well?"

"Or maybe... Monique, call that number and ask for Grace Rossi. I've got a hunch it's his sister."

She pressed the redial button again. The phone rang a couple of times, then a man answered.

"Is Grace Rossi there, please?"

"Na, she's out right now."

"Oh, is this her husband?"

"Na, she ain't married."

"Well, would you please tell her Carol phoned?"

"Ya, sure."

Monique put down the receiver. "I think we've found him."

Chapter Eight

From the time they got to New Orleans International until their flight actually departed, Ben was antsy as hell. Knowing you couldn't get a gun through security, he'd packed it in a small suitcase—along with the snubby he'd gotten hold of for Monique. And even though checked luggage wasn't X-rayed, he'd still been half expecting a dozen cops to suddenly surround them.

But once the plane took off and they left New Orleans behind, he started to relax. And after they arrived at La Guardia, he actually began thinking Lady Luck might be with them.

Among the *G. Rossis* listed in the Brooklyn phone directory was one with a number that matched Grace's, so finding her address wasn't even a minor challenge. And getting there was a simple taxi ride.

She lived just off Bedford Avenue, in a modest low-rise apartment building with an old-fashioned intercom that showed both the apartment number and occupant's name beside the buzzer.

"G. Rossi, two-twelve," he said, his heart beating a rapid tattoo as he gazed at the number. He was so close to Sandor Rossi he could almost smell the little bastard.

"I wonder if Rossi will recognize me with my disguise," he added while they waited for someone to come in or out. "He doesn't know me *well*, but he does know me."

Monique glanced at him, her gaze flickering from the baseball cap pulled low on his forehead to his growth of beard, then down over his bomber jacket, jeans and sneakers.

"I doubt he'll recognize you. You look more like a Yankees fan in terminal need of a shave than anything else."

He grinned. That was a hell of a lot better than looking like an escaped con.

When a woman with a little girl opened the door on their way out, he politely held it for them. Then he ushered Monique inside. They hurried up the stairs and along the second-floor hallway.

"Okay, you're on," he said, flattening himself against the wall beside the door and handing her the leather case. "That makes a great prop."

She gave him a nervous smile, then patted both her wig and the snubby in her coat pocket. Finally, she knocked.

Ben heard footsteps in the apartment, followed by silence while someone was undoubtedly looking out at Monique. Eventually a woman said, "Yes?"

"Avon lady," Monique told her.

"Sorry, I don't need nothin' right now."

"Oh, then just let me give you a free sample of our newest fragrance. You'll absolutely love it. It's the most wonderful product the company's ever brought out."

"Well...all right."

Ben held his breath while he listened to Grace Rossi slide the chain and unlock the door. The instant she opened it he wheeled into the doorway—grabbing her by the arm and slapping one hand over her mouth.

Within three seconds he and Monique were inside the apartment. The door was closed again and Grace was backed up against the wall and staring at him with the look of a woman certain she was about to die.

"Listen," he whispered to her. "I've got a gun, but nobody's going to get hurt if you do what I say. I just want to talk to your brother."

Part of the living room was visible down the short hallway ahead of them, its TV tuned to a loud cartoon show, and before he uttered another word, a man called from it. "Grace? Who was at the door?"

"That's Rossi," Ben said quietly, glancing at Monique. "Cover her."

Monique gingerly took the snubby from her pocket and pointed it at Grace.

"Not a sound when I let you go," he said, slowly taking his hand away from her mouth.

He unclipped the Walther from his belt, then walked down the hall, quickly stepped into the living room and targeted Sandor Rossi.

Even though it was February, the guy was sitting around in only a tank top and sweat shorts, so he clearly wasn't packing heat. For a split second he simply stared at Ben, then he went pale.

"Who are you?" he sputtered. "What do you want?"

"You don't recognize me? Maybe you should have looked more closely when I was sitting at the defense table."

"Oh, jeez! Ben!"

"Right, but take it easy. Everything's going to be cool as long as you tell me who The Nose is."

"Oh, jeez, I was only tryin' to help."

"Yeah, sure. So help. Who is he?"

Beads of sweat had appeared on Rossi's forehead.

As he wiped them away, Ben said, "I'm counting. And if you're not talking by the time I reach ten, I'll shoot you in the knee then work my way up."

"I...okay, Ben, okay. I'm gonna tell you the God's truth here. The Nose is nobody. No, that's not exactly what I mean. I mean he's a dead man. Died last year. Carmine Franco."

Ben mentally pictured Franco. He'd come to the house a few times, years ago, when he'd had business with Ben's father. But even though Franco was part of the Dixie Mafia, he'd been an old man when he died. He hadn't done much "business" in years.

"I don't buy that," Ben said at last. "Why would Franco have wanted my father dead? Why would he have framed me?"

"He didn't."

"Then why the hell are you talking about him? Who *did* set me up?"

"Ben, I don't know."

"Look, you keep playing games with me and I swear you'll be as dead as Franco."

"I…listen, I'm not playin' games. God's truth. I'm just tryin' to explain that I don't have a clue who popped your parents. Or who set you up for the fall. I don't know a damn thing! Sayin' Franco was behind what went down was just a plan I came up with."

"A plan?"

"Yeah, I mean, he was dead, so what was the harm? See, I figured if I put the blame on somebody else they'd let you out. I knew all along you wasn't guilty and—"

"Sure you did," Ben snapped, so much anger and frustration building inside him he could hardly contain it.

He'd been positive Rossi would have the answer he wanted. But either the creep was a damn good actor or he was telling the truth. And if he really *didn't* have a clue, this trip had been nothing but a waste of precious time.

"Ben, like I said, I was tryin' to help you. The plan was gonna get me some cash and get you outta Angola, too."

"You didn't give a rat's ass about getting me out of Angola, so what's with the cash? Who paid you and for what?"

"To tell what I knew. To help you get a retrial."

"But you just said you didn't know a thing!"

"Ben?"

Monique's voice startled him and he glanced to his left. She was still holding her gun on Grace, but they'd come into the living room.

"What?" he said, taking a step back so he could see Monique and keep an eye on Rossi at the same time.

Her expression, he realized after a second, was telling him to chill out.

"We're not in any hurry," she said quietly. "So why don't you let him start at the beginning and tell you the whole story."

Exhaling slowly, Ben told himself she was right. He'd be better off trying to calm down and letting the bastard talk. If he knew *anything* useful, it should come out.

"Okay," he said, focusing on Rossi again. "Let's hear it from the beginning."

"Think you could stop pointin' those guns at us first?"

Ben gestured Grace to go sit on the couch beside her brother, then lowered the Walther to his side.

Rossi immediately looked less like a frightened rodent, but Grace was obviously still scared spitless. She eased onto the very end of the couch—as far away from her brother as she could get.

"Well," Rossi began, "the first thing is I knew all along you wasn't guilty."

It was the second time he'd said that, and even though he was probably lying it made Ben's pulse quicken.

"See, I saw you at Maria's. Just before the hit went down in the restaurant."

"What?"

Rossi nodded rapidly. "I did. I delivered somethin' to Dominick that mornin'. And I was hangin' around 'cuz he wanted me to do somethin' else for him later. So your Aunt Rose said would I mind goin' and droppin' some pictures off to Maria—in the meantime, like."

Ben flashed back to that day. He'd gone to Maria's to help her plan a party for their parents' anniversary. And when he'd arrived, she'd been looking at pictures Dominick had taken at a recent family gathering.

"I was just gettin' back in my car," Rossi continued, "when you pulled up and went into Maria's buildin'."

"Are you serious?"

"God's truth."

"Then why on earth," Ben said, trying not to sound half as furious as he felt, "didn't you tell the cops that?"

"I...I was too scared to open my mouth at first. See, after I left Maria's I went back to Dominick's. So I was there when the stuff about the murders came on the TV. And Dominick went so nuts he kicked in the screen.

"The announcer was saying you'd done it, Ben, and I swear if you'd walked into that house Dominick would've strangled you with his bare hands. And you know how he goes when he's in a rage. So I was scared that if I started sayin' it wasn't you he'd turn on me."

"But you could have told the cops later! You could have come forward and testified! Your story would have backed up Maria's. Dammit, Rossi, you'd have kept me out of Angola!''

"No, that jury didn't believe Maria, so they sure as hell wouldn't have believed a two-time loser like me."

Staring at Rossi, all Ben could think was that if he really was a killer there'd be two more dead men in the world. Because right now he was feeling just the way he'd felt when he'd seen Spook grab Monique back in the swamp.

"Ben?" she said.

He looked at her.

"Rossi did what he did. We can't change that. So let's just get the rest of the story. What,'' she went on, turning to Rossi, "made you eventually come forward? Why did you contact Ben's lawyers and help get him the retrial?"

"Because I thought up the idea of pointin' the finger at Carmine Franco. So it wasn't just gonna be me sayin' I saw Ben at Maria's. I knew that wouldn't be enough. But I figured that sayin' I knew who was really behind the murders was."

"But…" Monique paused, as if trying to get all the details straight in her mind. "I didn't hear everything you said at the start,'' she finally went on. "But there's absolutely no truth to the part about this Carmine Franco? It's a total fabrication?"

"A what?"

"She means did you make the whole thing up,'' Ben snapped.

"Oh. Yeah.''

"Why?" Monique said.

"Because he figured it was a way of getting money," Ben muttered.

"From whom?"

That question, Ben realized as she asked it, had gotten lost among all the others.

"From whom?" He echoed her words—then leveled his gun at Rossi when the weasel merely shrugged.

Grace cringed into the corner of the couch.

Rossi quickly said, "Okay, okay. I got money from your sister. God's truth."

Ben nodded. He'd suspected Maria had been behind bribing Rossi, but when she hadn't said anything about it he'd decided not to ask.

"I told her I'd seen you that day," Rossi was going on. "Told her I knew Carmine Franco had set you up."

"And you said you'd tell your story to my lawyers for a suitable price. You're scum, Rossi, you know that?"

"But you changed your mind," Monique pressed on, cutting Ben off before he could vent any more of his anger. "Why?"

Rossi shrugged again, then glanced at Ben and clearly decided another fast answer would be a good idea. "I got told to. In no uncertain terms."

"Who told you?" Ben demanded. Finally, they were getting somewhere.

"Well…you're not goin' to like this, but it was Dominick. See, I was figurin' that after so much time he'd be okay with what I was doin'. Maybe even be glad to find out his nephew hadn't really murdered his own parents. But I was wrong.

"When he heard I'd helped get you a retrial, I thought he was gonna kill me. He told me you murdered his brother and prison was where you belonged. Said you should rot there for the rest of your life."

Ben exhaled slowly, disappointment flooding him. They weren't getting anywhere, after all. It wasn't whoever had set him up that had made Rossi back down, it was Dominick.

And the fact he had wasn't exactly surprising. Dominick DeCarlo wasn't a man of either compromise or reason. He hadn't spoken a word to Ben since the murders. And he hadn't spoken to Maria, either—except to call her every name under the sun for swearing Ben had been with her that day.

As far as Dominick was concerned, Antonio and Bethany DeCarlo had been gunned down by their own son. And once Dominick believed something, it might as well be carved in stone.

"See," Rossi continued, "Dominick *knew* Carmine Franco didn't have no grudge against your father. So he didn't believe that part of my story. And he didn't believe the part about me seein' you at Maria's, neither. He figured she just put me up to sayin' that—to get the retrial. And he told me if I swore in court that I'd seen you, I'd be dead before the day was out."

When Ben glanced at Monique, he could see his own thoughts mirrored in the brown depth of her eyes. And he could hear her silently asking the same question he was. *Where on earth do we go from here?*

5:51 p.m.

BEN WAS AS QUIET during the taxi ride from New Orleans International to the apartment as he'd been during the rest of the trip back from New York. He just didn't feel like talking, and Monique had given up trying to make him.

Tracking down Sandor Rossi had gotten him absolutely nowhere. And despite the fact he'd threatened both Rossi and Grace with death if they opened their mouths, he knew Rossi would seriously consider tipping off the cops. He'd find the lure of that reward money awfully hard to resist.

Of course, Rossi didn't have a *lot* of information. All he knew was that Ben had been in New York. And that he'd grown a beard.

But if Rossi *did* call the cops, he'd be sure to mention Ben had a woman with him. And that would mean they'd no longer be looking for a man on his own.

When the cab pulled up in front of the apartment, he told himself to stop worrying about what other people might do and concentrate on what *he* was going to do.

He still hadn't figured that out. But with any luck Farris Quinn had learned something that would help. Or maybe some of Dezi's digging had paid off.

As soon as they got up to the apartment, Ben turned on the cell phone. It rang immediately—a mechanical voice telling him to check in for messages.

While Monique took off her Cleopatra wig and shook her own hair free, he called the message center.

Both Maria and Dezi had phoned, but neither had anything new to report.

There was a third message, though. From Farris Quinn. And that was enough to start Ben's adrenaline pumping.

"Anything?" Monique said.

He nodded. "Farris Quinn called."

She moved nearer as he punched in Quinn's number, and when it began to ring he wrapped his arm around her waist. She leaned into him, so soft and warm against him it almost brought tears to his eyes.

They hadn't been together long, but he felt as if they knew each other inside out. And of all the things he'd lose if he failed at what he was trying to do, she was by far the most important.

"Farris Quinn," the reporter answered.

"It's Ben DeCarlo. I got your message."

"Right. And I got you some information."

His adrenaline pumping harder, he said, "Great."

Monique eased away and sat down on the couch, not taking her eyes off him.

"Well, I wouldn't go as far as *great*," Quinn was saying. "There's not much, but I did get a little background on Felicia Williams. She was a cocktail waitress who'd worked in a few of the sleazier joints in the Quarter. The last one was the Misty Bayou, over on Decatur. The cops talked to people there, but she was off work the night she was killed and nobody knew anything."

"But have the cops got any clues? Any suspects?"

"They don't have much. They aren't exactly busting their butts on this one. Since they've been trying to catch up with *you,* any cases that aren't high profile haven't been getting much attention.''

"So they've got nothing?'' Ben said, a feeling of frustration settling heavily in his chest.

"I didn't say nothing. I said not much. Felicia was in a strip club the night she died—a joint she waitressed at a year or two back. It's called the Twinkle and it's over on—''

"I know it,'' Ben said.

"Oh? You know the owner, too?''

"Yeah, Danny made a point of meeting me because I own the Crescent Wine Cellar. He seemed to think that gave us something in common.''

Quinn laughed his short, barking laugh. "I'd say the only similarity between your place and his is that they both sell wine.''

"Well, I'm not sure the stuff Danny Dupray sells actually qualifies as wine. But if Felicia was in his place that night maybe the murderer was there, too.''

"That's possible, but not likely. See, for some reason she decided to walk home from the Twinkle, even though it was late and she lived way over on Iberville.''

"That's a bit of a hike.''

"Right. But she almost made it. The alley her body was found in was only half a block from her apartment. So if someone had followed her from the Twinkle, they'd have probably killed her nearer to it.''

"Yeah, I guess that makes sense.''

"At any rate, the cops talked to Danny Dupray and his staff, but nobody there knew anything, either. So they've pegged the murder as just another thrill kill.

"But there's one other thing you might be interested in. Felicia had a psychic's card in her purse. A woman named Cheryl Tremont who works out of her apartment on St. Philip. Her number's 555-8342."

"Did the cops talk to her?" Ben asked, jotting that down.

"Uh-huh, but she didn't talk back. Told them her conversations with clients are privileged—like a lawyer's. And I gather they didn't care enough to argue about it. So...I'm afraid that's it. That's all I've got for you."

"It's more than I had five minutes ago, so thanks. And I'm not forgetting about that story."

"I'm not, either, DeCarlo. I'll be expecting to hear from you again. Bye."

"Bye." Ben clicked off, then sat down on the couch beside Monique and quickly filled her in.

"Do you think the police are right?" she asked when he finished. "That Felicia's murder was just a thrill kill? That it *wasn't* meant to keep her from meeting you the next day?"

"I don't know," Ben said wearily. "I guess it *could* have been a coincidence, but I've still got a feeling it wasn't."

"Then we've got two leads to check out, right? The psychic and the people at the Twinkle."

"Well, the psychic's definitely worth a try. But Danny Dupray and his people apparently don't know anything."

"Or maybe the police just didn't ask them the right questions. I mean, if they haven't given the case much attention..."

Ben shook his head. "I can't go and talk to Danny Dupray. Even with a beard and glasses he'd recognize me. And in addition to owning one of the sleaziest joints in town, he's a police snitch. I might just as well call the cops, myself, as go to see him."

"Then I'll go."

"Uh-uh. I don't want you anywhere near that place."

"Then what about Dezi?"

Ben shook his head. "He threw Dupray out of the Crescent one night, so if Dezi showed up at the Twinkle, Dupray would spit in his face."

"Ben," Monique said quietly, "if neither you nor Dezi can go there, that only leaves me or Maria."

"That leaves no one. I wouldn't let either of you get within a block of Danny Dupray. I'll give this Cheryl Tremont a call and we'll both go see *her.*"

"What if she knows who you are?"

"Why would she? I've never even heard of her."

"Ben, she's a *psychic.*"

That gave him a moment's pause. But he didn't really believe in psychics. He just thought Felicia might have said something useful to the woman. So before Monique could say another word, he punched in the number Quinn had given him.

The call was picked up by an answering machine. "Hello, this is Cheryl Tremont. If you'd like to make an appointment, please leave your name and number and I'll return your call as soon as possible."

"The name is Dick Rogers," he said, then rattled off the number. "And it's urgent that I talk to you.

So please call me as soon as possible—regardless of the time."

"She's not likely to phone back tonight," Monique said as he put down the cellular.

"Why not?"

"Because it's the last weekend before Mardi Gras. And you told me *everybody* spends the entire weekend celebrating. She'll probably be out late."

"I told her that didn't matter."

"I know. But even when you say regardless of the time, people don't phone if they think it's too late."

"*She* might. If she's really psychic, she'll know just how important it is."

"Very funny," Monique said, lightly punching his arm. "But I still don't think she'll get back to you tonight. So instead of sitting around wasting time, we could go to the Twinkle and—"

"No way."

"If you take the phone with you, she'll get you if she *does* call. And I could go into the club while you hung around right outside, and—"

"No way, Monique," he said more firmly.

"But I've thought of a plan."

"I don't want to hear it."

She gazed at him for a moment, then snuggled closer. And when he wrapped his arm around her she rested her head on his shoulder.

He sat breathing in the clean, fresh smell of her hair mingled with the intoxicating scent of her perfume. She was crazy if she figured they'd be wasting time by staying right here in the apartment all night.

"Ben?" she murmured.

"Uh-huh?"

"If I was in trouble, would you help me?"

"Of course."

"Why?"

"Because I love you," he whispered, kissing her.

"And I love you. That's why I want to go to this Twinkle club. And what's Danny Dupray going to do to me in a public place?"

"No, Monique. Absolutely not."

"Well...at least just listen for a minute, because the more I think about this plan, the better I like it."

Chapter Nine

Saturday, February 8
8:47 p.m.

The cobblestone streets of the Quarter were so crowded it took ages to walk the half dozen blocks along Royal. People were milling in and out of restaurants and bars, clustering around street entertainers, and simply wandering aimlessly—absorbing the atmosphere of Carnival.

None of them gave Monique and Ben more than a passing glance, but she always felt self-conscious wearing her wig. And she knew Ben was anxious.

Between light spilling from the buildings and its neon signs, the Quarter was brightly lit. And even with his Yankees-fan-in-terminal-need-of-a-shave disguise, there was always a chance they'd run into someone who knew him well enough to recognize him.

"That's it up ahead," he finally said, pointing down Dumaine as they turned the corner.

The Twinkle, which had clearly started life as a movie theater, put Monique in mind of one of the more unsavory stretches of Manhattan's Forty-second Street. On the club's marquee, running lights circulated around names of such strippers as Buxom Babbette and Candy Box.

"I really don't like this idea," Ben muttered, squeezing Monique's hand.

"I'll be fine," she told him. But by the time they reached the front of the club, where the sound of its music boomed out at them, she was having serious doubts about the wisdom of going in.

"You can still change your mind, you know," he said.

As tempting as that thought was, she shook her head. "All I'm going to do is ask a few innocent questions."

"It's who you'll be asking them to I don't like. Just remember I'll be right here if you need me."

"Don't be so right here that you're conspicuous." She gave him a quick kiss. Then, forcing a smile, she turned and walked into the Twinkle.

It was loud, dark, smoky, and full of men. Aside from the stripper on stage and a couple of barely dressed young waitresses, she was the only woman in the place.

A few of the customers glanced at her, but when they saw she was fully clothed they turned their attention back to the runway.

"Cover's ten bucks," a man said, materializing beside her. He was bald and muscular, with three hoop earrings in his left ear and a tattoo on his arm.

"I'm not staying. I'm just looking for someone."

Instead of asking who, the bouncer simply turned

to the man who'd walked in after her and repeated his ten bucks line. A moment later, though, one of the waitresses noticed her.

Quickly, Monique headed over. "I'm looking for Danny Dupray."

"Sorry, he's not hiring."

"No, I don't want a job. I just need to talk to him."

"I'd have to tell him what it's about."

"Felicia Williams. She was my sister."

"Oh...you poor thing." The young woman's tired expression softened, making her look both prettier and genuinely sympathetic. "I knew Felicia, and I was here the night she... We talked a little and... What's your name?"

"Anne."

"Well, you just come with me, Anne. Danny's in the back."

Monique followed along past the runway, which was tackily adorned with tiny blinking white lights, and on into the back of the building where the sound of the music wasn't as deafening.

"Yeah?" a man said when the waitress knocked on a door.

She pushed it open, revealing a messy office and a man sitting behind a desk. He was thin and pale, as if he never saw the light of day, and his features were so sharp that—even though Monique knew it was a crazy thought—they seemed downright dangerous.

"Danny," the waitress said, "this is Anne, Felicia Williams' sister. She just wants to talk to you for a minute."

"Felicia's sister." Danny eyed Monique's dark

wig, then his gaze drifted appraisingly to her Alfred Sung trench coat.

His blue eyes were dead, and his scrutiny gave her the same creepy-crawly feeling that Spook's had.

"You don't look like Felicia," he said at last.

"No, we took after different sides of the family."

"Ah. Well...I'm real sorry about what happened. We're all real sorry, aren't we, Barb?"

The waitress nodded, then turned to go.

"Could you stay a minute?" Monique asked quickly. "I mean," she added to Danny, "as long as it's okay with you. Barb mentioned she was talking to Felicia that last night, and anything anyone can tell me..."

Aside from which, even with a gun in her pocket Monique would rather not be alone with Danny Dupray. His words were smooth, but the vibes he was giving off warned her to be very careful—that he was a combination snake oil salesman and the snake itself, coiled to strike.

When Danny merely shrugged, Barb leaned against the wall and waited, absently tugging at the bottom of her brief outfit as if she was embarrassed to be wearing it.

"You see," Monique continued, "the police don't seem to have learned very much."

"I'm afraid that's the way it is with random murders," Danny said.

"I...yes, but I can't help thinking maybe it wasn't random. And that the killer could be found if... Felicia might have said something while she was here.

Anything you remember about that night might help.''

"Well, let's see," Danny said slowly. "She was a little tipsy, wasn't she, Barb."

"A little."

Danny smiled, displaying small, narrow shark's teeth. "I guess it was more than *a little*. At any rate, she was in a good mood. Said she'd come into some money. So I asked did she mean an inheritance and she said no. But that she wished she could tell us where it had come from because it was an unbeliev-able story."

"And she mentioned she was meeting some guy the next day," Barb put in. "I remember because she said she was helping him out with something—but that he didn't deserve it. That struck me as strange. I mean, I wondered why she'd help him if that's what she thought."

Felicia had been talking about Ben, Monique re-alized, glancing anxiously from Barb to Danny. Surely, though, there was no way either of them could have figured that out.

They didn't volunteer anything more, so Monique said, "And when she left? Did you notice anyone else leave at the same time? Anyone maybe following her?"

She held her breath, waiting for an answer. That was the big question. If they could find out who'd killed Felicia, who'd prevented her from meeting Ben…

But both Danny and Barb were shaking their heads.

"And there's nothing else you remember?"

"Not really," Danny said. "Except that she was determined to walk home rather than take a taxi. Said the air would clear her head."

"I told her not to," Barb murmured. "Everyone knows how dangerous the Quarter is at night, but she wouldn't listen. She was… Well, you know how stubborn she was, Anne."

Monique nodded, wishing she could think of a final magic question that would at least give her *something*. Otherwise, Ben was going to be awfully disappointed.

"Well," Danny said, "I'm sorry we can't be more helpful, but Barb's got to get back to work and I…" He waved his hand over the papers on his desk.

"Yes, of course. Thank you both for your time."

Feeling like a complete failure, she followed Barb out of the office and closed the door.

The waitress silently led the way back down the hall, then stopped outside the ladies' room and glanced both ways. "Come in here for a minute," she whispered, hustling Monique into the dingy washroom.

"If Danny knew I was telling you this he'd kill me," she said quietly. "He told me to keep my mouth shut about it, and I did with the police. But Felicia was my friend and…"

"And?"

"She didn't just *tell* us she'd come into some money. We saw it. Like Danny said, she was kind of drunk. And when she opened her purse to get something an envelope fell out. She grabbed it up right away, but we both saw it was full of hundred dollar bills. A lot of them, Anne. I'd say three or four thousand bucks. And then..."

"Yes?"

"After she left, Danny headed straight to his office. And I had to ask him about something, so I went there just a minute or so later. But I stopped outside the door because he was talking on the phone—about Felicia."

"Felicia," Monique repeated, her pulse racing.

Barb nodded. "I didn't hear enough to be sure exactly what the story was. But later he came up to me and said that if anyone ever asked about that envelope I should pretend I didn't know what they were talking about. And I don't think it was in her purse when they found her body. I mean, the police didn't say a word about it, so I can't help wondering if maybe Danny..."

"Phoned someone to tell them Felicia was walking home with a lot of money," Monique slowly concluded.

Barb nodded. "Then, if the guy tried to mug her and she fought him, maybe that's why she ended up dead."

"And Danny knew where she lived? The direction she'd be walking, I mean?"

"Sure. From when she used to work here. She mentioned she was still in the same place—the same old dump, as she called it. Only now that she had some money, she was thinking of moving. But, look, I've got to get back out front." Barb glanced anxiously at the door.

Monique rested her hand on the woman's arm.

"Thank you for telling me this. And is there anything else you remember? Anything at all?"

"No, I'm afraid not." The waitress turned toward the door, then hesitated and looked back. "Actually, there *is* one other thing. I don't know why it slipped my mind. Guess 'cuz I'm nervous about what Danny would do if he found out I told you. But the envelope wasn't plain. It had a company's name and address printed on it—one of those fancy, advertising kind of envelopes, you know?"

"And the company was?"

"Well, not exactly a company. It was a bar. The Crescent Wine Cellar. That place Ben DeCarlo owns."

11:14 p.m.

THE PHONE CALL TO DEZI simply confirmed what Ben and Monique had been assuming.

"I made a hell of a bad choice in hiring her, didn't I," Dezi muttered. "But it never occurred to me she'd go off drinking with that money in her purse."

"Hey," Ben said, "when you're paying someone to help a convicted murderer escape, you don't have the cream of society to choose from."

"Yeah, well…"

"Don't worry about it. You're busy," he added, hearing the background noise from the Crescent.

"Yeah, the joint's jumping, so I'd better go. It's tough managing a bar when the owner's never around."

"Very funny." Saying goodbye, Ben sat down on

the couch beside Monique and put his arm around her. "It's exactly what we figured. Dezi gave Felicia the money earlier that evening. So she obviously went off to celebrate and ended up at the Twinkle."

Monique slowly shook her head. "It's ironic, isn't it. If Dezi had chosen someone else, someone who hadn't gone to Danny Dupray's club and ended up getting killed, you and I wouldn't be together now."

"Are you glad we are?"

"Do you have to ask?" she said, giving him a little smile. "I wish Felicia wasn't dead, but I wouldn't want to wish any of the rest away."

He drew her close and kissed her, wondering how he could have gotten so lucky—and trying to ignore the fact that what they'd found together could be snatched away at any second.

"It must be bedtime," he finally murmured. The way her body was pressed against his made it impossible to think about anything but making love with her.

She smiled again, then said, "Almost. I just want to talk about Danny for a minute, about exactly what his game was. Do you think it was simply what the waitress guessed? That he let someone know Felicia was a prime candidate for a mugging? And when she resisted the mugger killed her?"

"No, my money's on the other possibility. When Danny saw that envelope from the Crescent, I'll bet he put two and two together. I mean, everyone assumed the jury would arrive at its verdict right away. So Danny concluded that *I* was the guy Felicia was supposed to help the next day. And if he called someone who didn't want her to, we'd have a far more likely explanation for why she ended up dead.''

"But if he called this *someone*... You really think Danny knows who set you up? Who had your parents killed?''

Ben wearily shook his head. "I'm sure not ruling it out. He's a police snitch, but he works the other side too, so he knows an awful lot about what goes on in this city.''

"Then we've got to find out exactly what he *does* know. If he—''

"The question is how," Ben said, that familiar feeling of frustration back in his chest. "If anyone started asking him questions about me, he'd tell this *someone*. Plus, he'd let the cops know, too, and get paid off twice. So I just don't see how we can—''

The phone began to ring and Ben gestured to Monique to pick up. They'd given the number to enough people that he could no longer assume it was either Dezi or Maria.

Monique answered it, then handed it over, whispering, "Cheryl Tremont.''

"Ms. Tremont," he said, "thank you for calling back.''

"I hope it's not too late.''

"No, I'm glad to hear from you. I have a problem, and I've been told you're the woman I should talk to about it.''

"Aah. And your message said it was urgent.''

"Yes, it is.''

"Well, I don't take appointments on Sundays, but I can see you on Monday morning if that—''

"Ms. Tremont, it's *extremely* urgent. And I'd be happy to pay double your normal rate if we could get together tomorrow."

"I see. In that case, shall we say ten in the morning?"

"Ten would be great. And I really appreciate it."

"Do you know where I am?"

"I know it's St. Philip Street, but I don't have the exact address."

When she gave it to him, he jotted it down, thanked her again, then hung up. "And you," he said, smiling at Monique, "told me I wouldn't hear back from her tonight."

"As I recall, I merely said it wasn't *probable*. How did she sound?"

"Businesslike. Although, I'm surprised she didn't ask who I was. Who Dick Rogers was, to be accurate. Or who'd referred me. It can't be entirely safe to just let strangers into her apartment."

"How many times do I have to point out that she's psychic," Monique teased. "She could tell over the phone that you're perfectly safe."

"I am, am I?"

He graced her with his best leer, which started her laughing. It made him reflect that they hadn't had many chances to laugh together. If they could just succeed at what they were trying to do, though, that would change.

"What are you thinking?" she asked.

Before he could tell her, the phone began ringing once more.

She answered it, then handed it to him again, this time saying, "Dezi."

"What's up?" Ben asked.

"I'm not quite sure, but it isn't good. I just had a call from Danny Dupray, and he was asking questions about Monique."

"What!"

"Calm down. I didn't mean he knows who she is."

"What?" Monique whispered. "What's wrong?"

Ben waved her off as Dezi continued. "He just said he thought I'd be interested to know a woman had been at his place asking about Felicia."

"And you said?"

"I said, Felicia who? But with seeing that damn envelope he's known about the connection all along. At any rate, he was just taking a shot in the dark that I might know something about Monique, because he realized she wasn't Felicia's sister. He said the woman who came to the Twinkle was a class broad who never in a million years grew up in the same family as Felicia."

"Dammit."

"Ben, it's not that bad. He was only sounding me out. And when I said I didn't know a thing, that was the end of the conversation. I just thought I'd better let you know."

"Yeah, thanks. But I sure don't like the thought of that sleazoid asking around about Monique."

"What?" she demanded again as he hung up.

"Danny Dupray thinks you're a class broad," he muttered.

"Oh, great, that certainly thrills me."

"Yeah, me, too."

After he filled her in on the rest of what Dezi had said, she shook her head. "I don't like the thought of him asking around about me, either. Why is he doing it?"

"Because his game is selling information—to the highest bidder. And he knows you were up to something, pretending you were Felicia's sister, so he was trying to find out what."

"So he could tell...?"

"Whoever would pay him the most."

"Ben, should I go and see him again?"

"No, the farther away you stay from him, the better."

"But if he—"

"Shh." Ben rested his fingers against her lips. "I don't even want to waste time talking about him, because all we'll do is go around in circles wondering what he's up to. And," he added, drawing her close, "I can think of something far more enjoyable than going around in circles."

Sunday, February 9
9:59 a.m.

CHERYL TREMONT WAS an attractive blond woman in her late thirties, and the moment Ben and Monique arrived at her apartment they discovered why she didn't worry about letting strangers in. She had a rottweiler the size of a small pony, and he appeared to be glued to her side.

"This is Rex," she told them. "Named for the

Mardi Gras king, not in the traditional Rex-as-a-dog's-name sense.''

"Hello, Rex," Monique offered.

The dog curled his lip, revealing king-sized teeth, so Ben passed on trying to make friends.

"Please sit down," Cheryl said, gesturing them to chairs at the table in the living-dining room.

She sat across from them, Rex still at her side, and eyed Ben for a long moment.

It made him anxious as hell. When he looked in the mirror these days, he barely recognized the bearded, dark-haired man staring back—so nobody who didn't know him would ever match him to any of the photographs the media had been using. Still, every time he was out of the apartment he felt uneasy.

"Your name isn't Dick Rogers," Cheryl said at last.

His mouth went dry, and the frightened glance Monique shot him didn't help any. What if Cheryl somehow realized who he was? Would she keep it to herself or not?

"It's okay," she went on. "I know some people are uncomfortable about consulting a psychic. But it would be better if you told me your real name."

"I'm afraid I can't," he said, desperately trying to figure out how to play this. "It might put you in a compromising position."

Cheryl slowly pushed her hair back from her face, her gaze still fixed on him.

He half expected her to tell him to leave, but she finally said, "All right, I can make do without a name, but I may not be able to sense much with that block between us.''

"Well, it's not really *me* I need you to sense something about. I...one of your clients, Felicia Williams, was murdered the night before she was supposed to meet with me. And I suspect someone killed her to prevent her from doing that. So I thought if she'd said anything to you, or if you'd sensed anything the last time she consulted you..."

"Are you aware the police came to question me about Felicia?"

"Yes."

"And do you know I didn't tell them anything?"

Ben nodded.

"Then why would I tell you?"

He racked his brain for an answer that might convince her to, but nothing came.

"Because," Monique said slowly, "whoever killed Felicia has probably killed before. And he'll undoubtedly kill again. If we learn who he is we can prevent that."

"I see. But when the police haven't learned who he is, what makes you two think you can?"

"We were hoping that if you'd talk to us about Felicia, something you say might help us."

Cheryl considered that, then said, "Normally I wouldn't do this, but I sense how important it is to you."

Ben reached for Monique's hand, thanking his lucky stars she was with him.

"Felicia was here the day she was murdered. And

there was an ugly aura around her that made me certain she was in danger.''

"You told her that?" Ben asked.

"Of course, and she said she already knew. But that she was being very well paid to do a job that involved only a little work, and she'd decided to take her chances."

"But you didn't sense who she was in danger from?" Monique said.

"It was a man, that's all I knew. You see, I can sense things about a person sitting right here with me, but very little about some stranger. All I knew was that Felicia was at risk, not who might harm her.

"You, though, are a different story," Cheryl continued, focusing on Ben. "Your life has been in turmoil for a long time, hasn't it?"

Taken aback, he simply nodded.

"Yes, and with you I can sense the source of your trouble. It comes from relatives. Members of your family have caused this turmoil."

"Aah…yes, that's right." His parents hadn't *intended* to be murdered, of course, but that *was* what had landed him in Angola.

"And you are still in danger. Both of you are," she added, glancing at Monique. "People are looking for you. And if they find you…"

"What?" Monique whispered. "What will happen? Do you know?"

Cheryl hesitated, then shook her head. "I'm not sure they *will* find you—only that there will be trouble if they do. But I know you're searching for someone. A man. And that you're going to locate him. But then…''

"Yes?" Ben pressed, his heart hammering.

"I…I'm sorry, but I can't be sure what will happen then. My strength doesn't lie in foretelling the future. I've never been able to see very far into it.''

"Can you sense *anything* more?" Monique said.

"No. Only that when you do find him… I sense *much* danger then. So be very careful.''

Chapter Ten

All Monique could think about as she and Ben walked back from Cheryl Tremont's apartment was how much she wished the woman had been able to see a little further into the future. They were going to find the man they were looking for, but then...

"I sense much *danger then."* The words refused to stop echoing in Monique's mind. How much was much? Enough to get them killed?

Clutching Ben's hand more tightly, she quickened her pace. She wanted to talk to him about everything the psychic had said, but the streets of the Quarter were full of people—some straight out of church, others who looked as if they hadn't been to bed in days—and she couldn't take the risk that the wrong person might overhear.

They finally reached their own building and hurried up to the apartment. When Ben closed the door behind them, she wrapped her arms around him and gave him a good, hard hug.

"What?" he whispered, stroking her hair. "What's wrong?"

"I'm afraid," she admitted.

"You've only decided to be afraid now? After all you've been through lately?"

"Don't tease," she murmured, gazing up into his eyes. "I didn't mean I haven't been afraid before. But I've been so focused on trying to find our mystery man that I wasn't thinking about what would happen if we actually did. And now that Cheryl's said we will…

"Ben, what's going to happen when we do? I mean, he certainly won't say, *Oh, you figured things out, so now I'll have to go to the police and turn myself in.*"

"Hey, take it easy. In the first place, just because Cheryl Tremont says something's going to happen doesn't mean it will. I wanted to see what she could tell us about Felicia, but I don't really believe in psychics. So I think we should be taking her predictions with a grain of salt."

Monique slowly stepped backward, out of his arms. "Ben, don't try to tell me you thought the woman was a hoax. She's psychic enough that she knew right away you'd given her a phoney name. And I saw how you reacted to what she was saying. You believed she knew what she was talking about."

"Well, okay, I'll admit she was pretty convincing. But people in her line have to be. Otherwise they'd never get any clients. But look, the important thing is that she gave me a wake-up call as far as you're concerned."

"What do you mean?" Ben's expression told Monique he was about to say something she wouldn't like.

"I mean that I've been insane to let you get more and more involved in this. You've got to back off before things *do* get too dangerous. So I want you to go home to Hartford or to your parents' or wherever. Then, when this is over, I'll—"

"Ben, do you love me?"

"Of course I do. I love you so much it scares me. But—"

"Stop, that's all I wanted to hear, because I love you just as much. Which means that if you think I'm leaving now, you *are* insane."

"But—"

"No! We are *so* close. Cheryl said her strength doesn't lie in foretelling the future, remember? That she's never been able to see very far into it. But she could see far enough to tell us we were definitely going to find the man we're looking for, so we can't be talking more than another day or two. And I'm certainly not leaving ten minutes before the final act."

"Monique, I—"

A knock stopped him mid-sentence. He turned and looked through the peephole, then quickly unlocked the door.

His sister hurried inside, looking as if she'd seen a ghost.

"What's wrong?" he demanded.

"I was waiting for you to get home—sitting in that café across the street, watching for you, because something's happened that I have to tell you about in person."

"Maria, *what's* happened?"

"Sit down," she said.

He reached for Monique's hand and headed over to the couch. "All right, we're sitting. Now, what's going on?"

Maria dropped into one of the chairs across from them. "Ben, I've been spending a lot of time in the attic over the past few days. I thought trying to clean it out would help keep my mind off things."

"Maria's back living in our parents' house," he explained, glancing at Monique. "We didn't want to sell it. Go on," he added, looking at his sister once more.

Wearily shaking her head, she said, "I don't know if I should even tell you this in the middle of everything else, but it came as such a shock to me that I—"

"Maria, for Pete's sake! Will you just spit it out?"

She gazed at him for a moment, then opened her purse and took out a large envelope. The edges were yellowed with age, and when she handed it to him it made the dry, crinkling noise of old paper.

There was no writing on it, Monique saw, nothing but an embossed name and address in the corner.

"Grenoble and Lancaster," Ben read the name aloud. "Attorneys-at-law. With a Las Vegas address. What the hell is this about?"

"Those are adoption papers. Mom and dad adopted you. In Las Vegas, right after you were born."

Ben stared at the envelope, feeling as if someone had punched him in the throat.

Monique silently rested her hand on his thigh.

"I'm sorry," Maria murmured. "Ben, I shouldn't have told you, should I. I just couldn't decide what was best. But I thought…"

"What?" he demanded.

"You're probably going to figure this is crazy, but all along we've assumed the killer was someone made up to look like you. And I started thinking, what if he actually *did* look like you—without even being made up. I mean, for all we know you have a brother."

"A brother who killed our parents? Is that what you're suggesting?" he said, trying to think straight. That couldn't be possible…and yet it was. Maybe a one-in-a million possibility, but a real one.

"Oh, Lord," Monique said.

He looked at her.

"The man outside the courthouse."

"What?" Maria asked.

"There was a man," Monique told her. "Right after the verdict came down I saw him standing outside the courthouse watching people leave. And he looked so much like Ben I thought it *was* him. It was one of the things that eventually started me believing Ben really could be innocent.

"Remember?" she added to him. "I told you I kept wondering if he could have been the real killer? Hanging around and waiting for the verdict—like an arsonist staying to watch a fire he's set."

Ben nodded. "I remember."

"But there's something I didn't wonder about until right now. Why would he have been made up like you that day? Just to stand outside a courthouse? Can you think of any reason?"

"No, not off the top of my head."

"Well I can't, either. And if he wasn't, then he's *got* to be a close look-alike."

"You mean," Maria said, "you think I might be right? That Ben really might have a brother?"

"A brother," Monique repeated. "Oh, Lord, Ben, remember what Cheryl Tremont said?"

"Cheryl Tremont?" Maria repeated.

"A psychic," Ben told her. "That's where we were this morning—seeing her," he added, not taking his eyes off Monique.

"She told you that *relatives* are responsible for all your trouble," Monique went on. "I took that to mean your parents, but maybe she was sensing that you're related to the killer."

"Wait a minute," Maria said. "This man you saw outside the courthouse. How could someone who looks so much like Ben be wandering around New Orleans? The first cop to see him, would have—"

"He probably left town faster than I did," Ben said. "I'll bet he was on his way before anyone even realized I'd escaped."

His gaze flickered to the address on the envelope and he stared at it for a moment. Then, his heart hammering, he pulled the papers from it and quickly skimmed them.

They'd been prepared by a Harold W. Grenoble, LL.B., and the details were clearly laid out. Adoption forms had been signed for a male infant when he was only two days old. The birth mother was a woman named Sally Windeller. And Antonio and Bethany DeCarlo had…

"They *bought* me." He looked over at Maria. "They paid this woman fifty thousand dollars for me. Plus her medical and legal bills."

"Ben?" Monique said softly. "That's the way private adoptions work. They didn't exactly *buy* you, they—"

"But why adopt a baby?" he interrupted, overwhelmed by a combination of shock, anger and curiosity. "Why not just have one of their own? They had Maria. I'm enough older to remember my mother being pregnant with her. So why did they adopt me?"

"There have to be people who know the answer to that," he went on, his thoughts racing. "They couldn't have had no baby one day and me the next without anyone being aware I was adopted."

"I could call Aunt Rose," Maria suggested. "She was so close to Mom that if anyone knows, she would."

"You think that would be safe? What if Dominick answers?"

"I'll hang up."

"He doesn't have one of those caller I.D. things?" Monique asked.

"They can't pick up cell phone numbers. And I wouldn't have to say anything about you, Ben," Maria went on. "Not that Rose would breathe a word, anyway. If she did, she'd have to admit to Dominick that she and I have been keeping in touch behind his back.''

"Just in case, though," Ben said, handing his sister the phone, "don't say a word about me. Just tell her you came across the papers and ask what she knows."

BEN HUNG ON EVERY WORD Maria said to Rose, but there weren't many of them. His sister was doing a lot more listening than talking.

"Well?" he asked the instant she clicked off.

"It seems unbelievable, but Rose didn't know. And she doesn't think *anybody* does."

"That's not possible!"

"No, I think it's true. Apparently, Mom desperately wanted a baby from the day she and Dad were married. But she couldn't get pregnant. Then, finally, she did. At least that's what she and Dad told people. But when she was about four months along—and not showing, Rose specifically said—the two of them went off on an extended vacation. They told everyone they wanted to tour Europe before the baby arrived.

"Then, supposedly, you came early. Were born in some little town in Switzerland. And they came straight home after that, you in Mom's arms."

He shook his head, feeling dazed.

"But why would they go to such extremes to hide the truth?" Monique asked. "Surely they didn't think there was any stigma attached to adopting a baby."

"You didn't know our father," Ben said. "I shouldn't be calling him that, though, should I. He *wasn't* my father. And Mom wasn't…"

When Monique rested her hand on his, he took a

slow, ragged breath, telling himself to put his emotional reaction to this on hold until later.

"What Ben meant about not knowing our father," Maria quietly explained, "is that he had the sort of macho mentality that said a man wasn't a man unless he was a stud. And I don't know if people got tested in those days, but if he knew the problem was on his side... Well, he'd have died before admitting he couldn't father children."

"But he *could*," Ben said. "He fathered you."

"I might have been a fluke, though. Maybe that's why they never had any more kids. Maybe they kept trying and couldn't. But that doesn't matter. The point I was going to make," Maria went on, looking at Monique, "is that Dad absolutely adored our mother, so—"

"*Your* mother," Ben muttered, unable to keep the words from slipping out.

"Ben...they were your parents, too. The only ones you ever knew. And that made you their son and me your sister. You aren't going to reject me as your sister, are you?"

"No, of course not. I'm just a little...shell-shocked."

"I know." Maria gave him a shaky smile, then looked at Monique once more. "At any rate, Dad absolutely adored Mom, so I guess when she wanted a baby so badly he agreed to adopt one. But only if nobody knew."

After Maria finished speaking, Ben sat staring at the Las Vegas address on the envelope again.

He was thirty-four years old. What were the odds

his birth mother still lived in the same city as she had that long ago?

And even if he could track her down, he might discover she'd had no other children—let alone one who'd walked into Augustine's and killed Antonio and Bethany DeCarlo.

But he had to find out.

Monday, February 10
10:19 a.m.

MONIQUE HADN'T WANTED to seem negative about this trip, so she'd been keeping her doubts to herself. But the idea of a brother nobody knew existed having been the man who'd murdered the DeCarlos... It seemed to her there were simply too many improbabilities in that scenario to actually make it hang together.

As the plane was descending toward Las Vegas's McCarran International, she finally said, "Ben? If you *do* have a brother, who knew about him?"

"Whoever hired him. Whoever wanted my father dead and me framed."

"But if nobody knew you were adopted...?"

"Somebody must have."

"So this person somehow knew the DeCarlos weren't your birth parents. And that you had a brother. And then paid him to..."

"To kill my father," Ben finished her sentence with a weary shrug. "Killers-for-hire are out there, Monique. You lived in New York long enough to know they're not rarities, and most of them are *some-*

body's brother. I'm not exactly thrilled by the thought that one of them might be mine, but...

"Look," he continued after a minute, resting his hand on hers, "I know this brother-as-murderer theory is a pretty remote possibility. But we're running damn low on leads."

She nodded, then sat gazing out the window as they landed, telling herself that a remote possibility was better than none at all.

But if Ben *did* have a brother, and he *was* the killer, then if they managed to track him down they were going to end up face-to-face with a murderer.

Not that they didn't have a plan for that eventuality. They'd checked a suitcase with their guns in it again. And in the big purse Maria had lent them were a tape recorder and a length of clothesline.

But the idea of getting a taped confession at gunpoint, then tying up a killer...

Every time Monique got to that part, shivers ran down her spine. What else could they do, though? Call the police and hold the guy at gunpoint until they arrived?

That obviously wasn't an option, because the police wouldn't just let them walk away with no questions asked. And once they realized who Ben was, they'd arrest him on the spot—and probably let the real murderer go, to boot.

No, however this played out, they were on their own.

Still dwelling on that unhappy fact, she followed Ben off the plane and into the terminal. While he waited at the baggage carousel, she headed for a bank of phones and started looking through one of the books.

But the luck they'd had finding Grace Rossi's address didn't hold. Not only wasn't there a single listing for anyone named Windeller, there were also no listings for either the law firm of Grenoble and Lancaster or any H. Grenoble, which made Monique fear the worst.

After a couple of guesses at what it might be called, she found a number for the law society. A helpful woman there checked her records and discovered that Harold W. Grenoble was simply retired, not dead.

"I'm not at liberty to give out his number," she said, "but if you'd like to give me yours I can contact him and ask him to call you back."

"I'm at a pay phone."

"I'll call him as soon as we hang up and explain that. I'm afraid it's the best I can do."

"Then I'll wait right here. And thank you so much." As Monique was saying that, Ben appeared at her side, holding the suitcase that contained their guns.

He stood absently rubbing his beard, then tugged his baseball cap down a little further.

"You know what I hate?" he said when she hung up. "That you're having to walk around with a guy who looks like a bum."

"I don't mind. You're just...it's the grunge look, that's all. And maybe it's still in style."

"Yeah. Maybe in some small town in North Dakota or some place."

She smiled, then said, "There was nothing under

Windeller. And Grenoble's retired and the law society wouldn't give me his number. But I've got someone contacting him for me, so with any luck he'll call right back.''

"Hey, you're getting awfully good at this stuff. Maybe you should think about becoming a private eye.''

"Maybe I should.''

"But you know what else I hate?'' he said, looking serious again. "That you're having to do everything.''

"There's no other way, is there. Even in Las Vegas, you can hardly expect people won't recognize the name Ben DeCarlo. Not when your case was at least as high profile as the Menendez brothers'.''

"Which means that if Grenoble... Monique, are we *sure* we're doing the right thing here? Even if he's forgotten all about the adoption and hasn't made a connection before this, when you show him those papers and he sees the names Antonio and Bethany *DeCarlo*, isn't he bound to realize it's *me* you're asking about?''

"Maybe he won't,'' she said, although she was certain he would. "He probably doesn't know that your parents named you Ben, so the last name *could* just be coincidental. And after all the time we spent trying to figure out what to do, this is the best plan we've come up with, isn't it.''

"I'm just afraid our best is pretty poor.''

"Well, he's the only potential link we've got to Sally Windeller. And even if he has his suspicions about me, what can he do?''

"Call the cops?''

"He wouldn't have much to tell them. Only that a woman came looking for information." Before Ben could say anything more, the phone rang.

She grabbed it, and when a man said, "Is that Anne Gault?" she offered up a little prayer of thanks.

Harold Grenoble sounded like a darling. And once she explained she needed to know something about one of his old cases he agreed to see her on short notice.

"I've got an appointment with him at twelve-thirty," she told Ben when she hung up.

"Good going!"

"And he said he's got a lot of his files stored in his basement. So if your mother used his services for anything else—something more recent, I mean, maybe he *does* have her current address."

"Anything's possible, but we'd better not start counting on it. The odds can't be very high that he'll know it. Hell, if she's married, he probably won't even know her current name."

"Maybe he will, though. After all, Cheryl Tremont said we'd definitely find the man we're looking for. So we've got to get a break soon."

"Only if Cheryl actually knew what she was talking about. And as I've said before, I don't have much faith in psychics."

Monique didn't reply. She knew as well as Ben did that Grenoble wasn't very likely to be any help, but he was all they had.

Ben draped his arm over her shoulders. "Come on. Let's just get an early lunch here, then grab a cab."

"Sure," she said, forcing a smile. "There's nothing I like better than airport food."

"You ought to try prison food," he muttered.

She pressed closer to him as they walked, refusing to dwell on the fact that they wouldn't be able to keep getting away with what they were doing forever. Or on the certainty that if they didn't get a break soon, Ben would end up back in Angola.

HAROLD GRENOBLE LIVED in one of the city's sprawling suburbs, far from the gaudy glitter of the famed Vegas strip. And while Ben waited at the corner of the street in their cab, Monique walked along to the man's house.

Somewhere in his seventies, he proved to be every bit as charming as he'd sounded on the phone, which at least made her feel a little less nervous.

"Now, what can I do for you, Ms. Gault?" he asked once they were seated in his study. "You said it was something about an old case."

She nodded. "My husband was adopted as a baby—a private adoption—and we've been searching for his birth mother. I have a name I think might be hers. And if it is, you handled the adoption."

"I see. And what you want from me is…?"

"The last address you have for her. Or anything that might help us find her."

"Aah. Well, in a case like this, assuming I *did* have any knowledge of her current whereabouts, I would have to contact her and let her know you and your husband are searching for her. Then, if she agreed to meet with you… But only if she agreed."

"I understand."

"And the name you have is?"

"Sally Windeller."

The strangest expression flickered across his face. "Then, I'm afraid I can't help you, Ms. Gault."

"But you arranged for the adoption," she said, telling herself to remain calm as she took the papers from her purse. "Look," she added, placing them on his desk.

He nodded, barely glancing at them. "I remember the case well, but I know Sally Windeller wouldn't have any desire to talk to you."

"How can you be sure?"

"Because Sally is my niece—my older sister's daughter. That's why I was the lawyer involved with the adoption. So I'm sorry you've come here for nothing, but—"

"Wait," Monique said, frantically trying to think of what to say. She was so near to getting the information that she simply *couldn't* let it slip through her fingers. If Ben's mother was this man's niece, he must know exactly where she was.

"Mr. Grenoble... I haven't been entirely honest with you."

"Yes, I realize that. The media has covered the most minute details about the DeCarlos' son. In fact, I've been amazed no reporter managed to discover he was adopted. And one of the things I recall is that he isn't married. Which, in reality, makes you...?"

"A friend." She blinked back tears, certain Grenoble was on the verge of throwing her out. "And I sincerely apologize for lying to you. But there's more to this than simply a search for a birth mother. It's absolutely *essential* I get in touch with Sally Windeller. It's a matter of life and death.''

"Life and death," he repeated.

She nodded, not able to come up with anything else that might help convince him.

He gazed across his desk at her while the clock on his wall ticked away the seconds. ''I'm not sure what to do here,'' he said at last. ''By rights, this should be Sally's decision to make. But I just don't think that putting her in the position of having to—''

"Mr. Grenoble... You're my only hope."

He eyed Monique for another minute, then said, ''All right, I'll tell you what I'm going to do. I'll give Sally a call and explain that you're sitting here in my office. But if she doesn't want to see you, that's the end of it.''

Without another word, Grenoble flipped open his personal directory and reached for the phone.

Chapter Eleven

"I still can't believe she agreed to see you," Ben said, squeezing Monique's hand as the taxi sped along the Las Vegas Expressway.

"I can hardly believe it, either. But don't get your hopes up too high, okay?"

He nodded, telling himself that was good advice. They still didn't know whether he even had a look-alike brother. But if he did, and if their long-shot murderer theory turned out to be fact, it would mean his brother was a cold-blooded killer.

Not wanting to dwell on that thought, he said, "Grenoble didn't say *anything* else about Sally Windeller?"

Monique smiled. "Do you think I'm holding out on you? I told you, I got the feeling she asked him to tell me as little as possible. Virtually all he did was give me the address and say it was a motel."

"But then you wondered about that and...?"

That made her laugh. "Honestly, Ben, you sound

like a little boy who's already been told the same story a dozen times. But when I wondered about it, he explained how her parents had made her invest the $50,000 at first, because she was only nineteen. But that a few years later, she used it to buy this Shilo Inn place.''

''She must have had guts, going into business for herself when she still couldn't have been very old.'' Nineteen when she'd had him, he reflected once more. Only a child herself.

His sister had been right, of course, when she'd said that the DeCarlos had been his *real* parents. Now that he'd had some time to work through his feelings, he realized the truth of that. And especially, Bethany DeCarlo had been his *real* mother.

Still, he couldn't help wondering if he looked like Sally Windeller. And about who his father was, and whether any of his grandparents were still alive. There were a host of other questions as well, but he wouldn't be getting the answers to most of them. Not today, at least. Today he had other priorities.

When the cabbie pulled off the expressway, Ben's adrenaline began to pump. He was dying to suggest that he hang in all the way to the Shilo, but made himself keep quiet.

As much as he wanted to meet the woman who'd given birth to him, and hear what she had to say first-hand, he knew it would be too risky.

Hell, it was dicey enough for Monique to be going in there. What if either Grenoble or Sally Windeller had called the cops—let them know that some friend of Ben DeCarlo's would be showing up to see Sally?

He told himself that hadn't happened. After all, the woman was his *mother*. Then he looked at Monique and tried to stop imagining her being interrogated by a team of detectives.

"The Shilo's just up the block," the cabbie said, glancing at them in the rearview. "You want I should let you out here?"

Ben nodded, and the man pulled over.

"Okay," Ben whispered to Monique. "If you spot a cruiser, or anything that even looks as if it *might* be an unmarked police car, tell this guy to keep going."

"I know," she whispered back. "I'm getting awfully good at this stuff, remember?"

He forced a smile and said, "Practice makes perfect, huh?" Kissing her, he grabbed the suitcase that contained their guns—then hesitated.

At the moment, though, Monique didn't need hers any more than he needed his. And taking them out of the case in front of the cabbie wouldn't be smart.

"See you in a few minutes," he said, sliding out of the taxi and trying to look nonchalant. But he wanted to go along with her so badly it was all he could do to keep his feet from moving when the taxi pulled away.

Once the cabbie headed off again, Monique smoothed her wig and gazed intently out at the parked cars they were passing—even though she probably wouldn't recognize an unmarked police car if it drove into her.

She took a deep breath as the taxi turned into the lot of the Shilo Inn. It was a relatively small and modest motel, but not the unsavory sort most people would never even consider staying at.

After checking that there were no suspicious-looking cars parked outside any of the units, she paid the driver and anxiously headed into the office.

A woman was sitting at a computer behind the counter, and when she glanced up she looked every bit as nervous as Monique felt. She was a little washed-out but still attractive, and she had deep blue eyes the exact color of Ben's.

"Ms. Windeller?"

"Actually, I go by Brooks. I was married for a few years, way back. Call me Sally, though. And you're Anne Gault, of course."

Monique nodded, feeling a twinge of guilt. Sally Brooks seemed like a nice woman, the kind who made people want to be honest with her.

"I'd invite you into the back," she said, gesturing toward a partially open door that led into living quarters, "but I'm here alone—with the phones and all."

"That's no problem. And I won't take much of your time. I just want to—"

"How is he?" Sally quietly interrupted. "My son."

"He's...Sally, he didn't do it. He's not a killer."

Sally gazed at her for a minute, then said, "Thank you for saying that."

"I'm not just *saying* it. Ben didn't murder Bethany and Antonio DeCarlo. Someone who looked like him did."

"If that's true," Sally murmured, "it must have

been so awful for him. First his parents dead. Then ending up in prison. Now on the run.''

"Yes. It hasn't been good. And I..."

Monique tried to ask the critical question but couldn't. The moment she did, Sally would know the real question wasn't simply did she have another son. It was did she have another son who might have committed the murders. There was simply no way of phrasing it that—

At the sound of the door opening, Monique glanced toward it—and her breath caught in her throat. Ben was walking into the office.

"Oh, my God," Sally whispered. "It's you."

Monique focused on her once more, certain she couldn't have instantly recognized Ben—particularly with his beard—unless she *did* have another son who looked incredibly like him.

"Sorry," he said, shrugging sheepishly when Monique turned toward him again. "But I could see there were no cops around, and only the two of you in here, and I couldn't resist."

Ben turned his gaze to Sally...to his birth mother. He simply stood there holding the suitcase and looking at her, his throat tight and a funny feeling in his chest.

It seemed so strange not to have met his own mother until now. But she *was* his biological mother. He had her eyes. And she had a cleft in her chin, just like his. He'd always wondered where that had come from.

"Hello," he said at last. "I just had to meet you."

She nodded, her face pale.

"Have you asked her yet?" he said to Monique.

"No."

"Then I will." His heart pounding in his ears, he made himself say, "Do I have a brother? One who looks a lot like me?"

His question hung for a long, tense moment. And then she shook her head. "I never had any more children, Ben. I'm sorry. I know what you were thinking."

He felt as if he was collapsing in on himself. He'd been trying not to count on this, but deep down he had been. And now...

Now what? This had been his final lead and it had led nowhere.

"Ben?" Monique whispered, moving to his side and reaching for his hand. "Ben, take it easy, we're not done yet. We'll figure some way of finding out what Danny knows."

Ben merely shook his head. Any more dealings with Danny Dupray would be just too risky. He sold information to too many people on both sides of the law.

And that meant they'd reached the end of the line. All Ben could hope now was that he'd be able to get to some corner of the world where he'd be reasonably safe, because he'd force the cops to shoot him before he'd go back to prison.

But even if he succeeded in making a future for himself somewhere, it couldn't be with Monique. He loved her too much to drag her into an entire lifetime of hiding out and constantly feeling uneasy. She'd already tasted that kind of existence in the witness protection program, and he knew how much she'd hated it.

He took one last look at his mother, then said, "I guess this is goodbye."

When she wiped her eyes, his own began to sting.

He quickly turned to leave, but at that exact moment a door somewhere else slammed and a man yelled, "Mom, I'm home early! And you're not going to believe what that bastard of a boss did to me!"

For a split second Ben froze. Then he frantically dug in his pocket for the key to the suitcase, wondering what lapse of sanity had kept him from taking the guns out at the damn airport.

Just as his fingers found the key, a man wearing a security company uniform—complete with gun and holster—stormed through the doorway from the living quarters. He stopped in his tracks and stared at Ben.

Ben stared back. It was like looking at himself, minus his beard and with his hair back to its natural color.

"Shee-it!" the other man said, drawing his gun. "If it isn't my long lost twin brother."

Twin. This man pointing a gun at him was his twin.

"Larry," Sally said sharply. "Larry, there's no need for that gun."

"No?" he snarled. "Well I think you're wrong. In there," he added, gesturing for the others to precede him into the living quarters.

Ben held back, hoping for a chance to heave his suitcase, but Larry gave a menacing wave with his gun and muttered, "Get moving."

Once they were all in the living room, Larry kicked the door to the office shut.

"Okay, Benny boy, put down that suitcase. Then you and your girlfriend go sit on the couch."

Ben set the case down and took Monique's hand. It was icy cold, and he knew she was petrified. He led her over to the couch, desperately trying to think of how they could get out of this. But as long as Larry was training his pistol on them, there wasn't much hope.

"Go get something to tie them up with," he ordered Sally, not taking his eyes off Ben and Monique.

"Larry, this is crazy. Just let them leave."

"What? So they can tell the cops they found someone who looks just like Benny boy? Make them think those eyewitnesses could have been wrong, and use his fancy lawyers to lay the blame on me? Get real."

"Then what are you going to do?"

"I'll take care of them. There's nothing for you to worry about."

"Larry, I—"

"Get me something!" he snapped. "There's some rope in the storage unit. Go down there and get it."

She hesitated for a second, then turned and fled.

"Twins," Monique murmured, gazing at Larry. "You said you're Ben's twin?"

"Yeah, lucky me, huh? She agrees to adopt her baby out. Then she ends up having twins and convinces her parents to let her keep one—to not even tell the DeCarlos there were two of us. And you know why she got to keep me?" he asked, eyeing Ben.

"No. Why?"

"'Cuz she could afford to. 'Cuz the DeCarlos were so damn rich they paid her fifty grand for you. Did you know that?"

"I just found out."

"Well I've known for a long time. She told me the whole story when I was a kid—except for *who* adopted you. I only discovered that a few years back.

"Fifty grand! You know how much money that was thirty-four years ago? Enough that she didn't have to worry about being in poverty if she kept me. So I got to grow up in this crummy joint while you were growing up in an effing mansion. Stupid bitch. And she figured I should be glad she decided to keep me."

"She did it because she loved you," Monique said quietly. "I'm sure she'd have kept both of you if she could have."

"Yeah? Well I don't figure she did me any favor. I coulda grown up in that mansion with Benny boy, here. If she'd told the DeCarlos about me, they'd have adopted the both of us. But the stupid bitch kept me. So I could slave my ass off around here while I was growing up, then get some dumb job and live a lousy life.

"See," he went on, scowling at Ben, "I don't have no fancy wine bar. And I don't have no fortune tucked away. In fact, as of this afternoon I don't even have a job. I got canned an hour ago. It's just a good thing this gun belongs to me, not them, huh? Otherwise I wouldn't even have it."

"Larry?" Sally said from the doorway.

Ben looked at her and stopped breathing. She

didn't have any rope, but she had a very large Magnum. And she was pointing it at Larry.

"What the hell do you think you're playing at?" he snapped, his gaze flickering her way.

"You're going to let them go."

"Like hell I am. Put that thing down."

Instead of doing as he ordered, she cocked the hammer. The quiet click sounded incredibly loud in the silence of the room.

Ben glanced from her to Larry, his heart in his throat, vaguely aware that Monique was holding so tightly to his hand she was cutting off his circulation. He gave a quick squeeze, then slowly drew his hand away from hers. If he got the slightest chance...

"You wouldn't shoot me," Larry told Sally. "I'm your son."

"So is Ben," she murmured.

When Larry gave her a long, furious look, Ben seized his chance. He threw himself across the room and tackled Larry. His gun exploded as they went down.

The sound was echoed by someone screaming, striking terror in Ben's heart. He knocked his brother cold with a single blow to the temple—a trick Dominick DeCarlo had taught him when he was just a boy—then he stuck Larry's gun into his waistband and looked across the room.

Monique was standing with her hand resting on Sally's shoulder. Sally was holding one arm with her other hand—blood oozing through her fingers.

"I'm all right," she told him. "I don't think it's too serious."

Ben eyed both women for a second, relief sweeping him, then he remembered Monique had a tape recorder and some clothesline in her purse.

"Bring me that clothesline you've got," he told her.

When she did, he quickly tied it around Larry's hands and feet. Then he strode across the room to Sally.

"It really *isn't* too bad," she said. "But what about Larry?"

"He'll wake up with one hell of a headache, but he'll be okay."

When Sally simply nodded, Ben exhaled slowly, feeling emotionally swamped. Then he put his arm around her waist and kissed her cheek. "Thanks," he whispered. "You saved our lives."

"You're my son," she said, blinking back tears. "But so is Larry. And what am I going to do about him? I think he really might have killed you."

"We've got to get you to a doctor. That's the first thing. After that, we'll figure out the rest."

Ben gagged Larry with a scarf of Sally's, then they left through the office. After locking the place up tight and flipping over the Back in 30 Minutes sign, he drove her Ford to a clinic not far from the Shilo.

While Monique and Sally went inside, he sat in the car trying to recall exactly what Larry had said earlier. Sally had told him to let them leave. And Larry had said...

"What? So they can tell the cops they found some- one who looks just like Benny boy? Make them think

those eyewitnesses could have been wrong, and use his fancy lawyers to lay the blame on me?''

That had been a long way from a confession of guilt. And Ben would have been a lot happier if Larry had admitted he'd been the one in Augustine's that day. As it was, he'd simply sounded like a paranoid who figured his brother was looking for a scapegoat. But Larry *had* to be the killer.

Didn't he?

One way or another, they were going to find out as soon as they got back to the Shilo. And then there was the other million dollar question. If Larry had been the shooter, who had known he existed and *planned* the murders?

3:48 p.m.

THE THREE OF THEM DROVE back from the clinic in silence, Sally curled up in the back seat cradling the arm that was now in a sling.

She was a little groggy from the painkillers the doctor had given her, but even if she hadn't been, Monique thought, there somehow seemed no point in talking about anything until they got their answers from Larry. And if the answers were what she was certain they'd be, she and Ben had succeeded.

Glancing across the front seat at him, she was almost afraid to believe they had. She'd fallen so deeply in love with him that if she couldn't be with him for the rest of her life...

She told herself not to even think about that. They'd found the real killer, so everything was going to turn out fine. No, she corrected herself as Ben turned into the Shilo's lot, everything was going to turn out wonderfully.

"What the...?" he muttered, pulling the car to an abrupt stop a good twenty feet from the motel's office.

Monique followed his gaze with her eyes and a queasy feeling began creeping around inside her. A teenaged boy was standing inside the office looking out at them.

"Oh, my," Sally said, sitting up in the back. "Oh, my, how did he get in?"

"Who is he?" Ben demanded.

"His name's Kevin, and he helps out after school most days. Cleans up around the lot, looks after the pool and things. But he doesn't have a key."

Ben was out of the car and racing for the office before Monique had her door open. Her heart pounding, she helped Sally out as quickly as possible—which wasn't too quickly given her sling. Then they headed after Ben.

"He's gone!" he said, turning toward them as they hurried into the office. "Larry's gone!"

Monique simply stared at him. His expression was dark and desperate, and she knew exactly what he was feeling. If they'd come this close, only to have their happy ending slip through their fingers...

As she swallowed over the lump in her throat, he wrapped his arm around her shoulders and pulled her close. She breathed in his comforting male scent, wanting to simply bury her face against his chest and make the rest of the world go away. Instead, she forced herself to look at Kevin and tune into what he was saying.

"Some guys mugged him, Sally! They knocked him out and took his gun and tied him up and everything. But I found him and untied him. See, when the office was locked I thought maybe you were just in back. So I went around the side. And when I looked in the living room window, there was Larry. So I...well, I'm afraid I had to break the window to get it unlocked. But then I just climbed in and untied him. So what happened to your arm?" he added, eyeing the sling.

"A little accident, that's all."

"Kevin, where did Larry go?" Ben demanded.

"I don't know exactly. He took off in his car after the muggers. I said we should call the cops, but he said he knew the guys who did it and he'd take care of things himself. I don't know for sure what he had in mind, but there was a gun sitting on a table in there and he grabbed it on his way out."

"My Magnum," Sally said. "I think I put my Magnum down on the table."

"Hey." Kevin eyed Ben curiously. "You look a lot like Larry, you know? I mean, except for your beard."

"He's Larry's cousin," Monique told the boy.

"Well, Kevin..." Sally said. "I'm afraid between hurting my arm and all this excitement I'd better lie down for a bit. So instead of working, you go on home now."

"Oh, I won't make any noise, I'll—"

"I'll pay you for your regular hours," Sally interrupted. "But you just go on."

"Uh…sure. If you say so." With a confused look on his face, Kevin backed out of the office.

"Lordy," Sally said as the door closed behind him, "what do you think Larry's going to do?"

Ben shook his head. "I don't even know what *I'm* going to do. I *had* to talk to him."

"Well, come into the apartment. There are some things we've got to discuss."

Monique and Ben followed her from the office to the living room, Monique's anxiety level sky-high. After Larry drove around for a while without finding them, wouldn't he come home again?

The thought of his arriving back made her stomach churn. And Ben must have had the same thought, because he unlocked their suitcase, handed her the snubby and clipped his own gun to his belt. Then he gave Sally the gun he'd taken from Larry.

She'd sat down on a chair and now she gestured toward the couch across from it. "Please sit. There are a few things I have to say."

Once they were seated, she said, "Ben, I apologize for lying earlier. About not having any other children. But when my uncle called and told me Anne was in his office asking about you—"

"It's actually Monique," she interrupted, feeling she *had* to be honest. "My name is really Monique LaRoquette and I was one of the witnesses to the DeCarlo murders. I testified against Ben, but now I know it wasn't him who killed them."

"I see." Sally slowly shook her head. "The world

is a very strange place, isn't it. The way things unfold. But getting back to my Uncle Harold's call, it took me so by surprise that I'd hardly thought of what was best to say by the time Anne…Monique got here.

"I followed your trials, Ben, so I knew your defense was that the killer had been someone who looked like you. And I realized that if you found out about Larry…

"Well, pretending there *was* no Larry just seemed the best idea all around. I mean, you'd eluded the police all this time, so I thought, ideally, you'd gotten away for good. And if you had, then *neither* of my sons would be in prison."

"Are you saying," Ben said slowly, "that Larry *should* be in prison?"

"Ben, I just don't know. But what's worried me for a long time is that he wasn't here in Las Vegas when the DeCarlos were murdered."

Ben's hand tightened around Monique's. Her heart began to beat faster.

"He told me he was going skiing in Lake Tahoe, but I have no way of knowing if that was true. Actually, I eventually tried to check, but there are so many places to stay in Tahoe, and the room might have been in someone else's name and… Well, the point is I couldn't find out for sure.

"There's only one thing I know that might be a clue. But it might be nothing at all."

"What is it?" Ben said. When he leaned forward on the couch, Monique could feel the tension emanating from him.

"Not long before those killings, a man phoned here

one afternoon. Larry wasn't home from work yet, and the man asked me to have him return his call. He didn't leave a number, though. He said Larry had it. And it was right after Larry phoned back that he told me he was planning on taking a few days off work and going to Tahoe.

"I assumed this man was someone he was going with or something, and I thought it was kind of strange that I'd never even heard his name before. But Larry rarely tells me any details about his social life, so I didn't really think much about it. Not until a year later, Ben—during your original trial, when I learned about your look-alike defense. It was then that I went back through my journal and checked to see exactly when Larry had been away."

"And it was definitely at the time of the murders?" Monique asked.

Sally nodded.

"And this man who called?" Ben said, his voice barely audible. "Do you remember his name?"

Monique closed her eyes and began to wish harder than she'd ever wished before.

"Yes, I wrote it into my journal at the time. His name was Danny Dupray."

Chapter Twelve

Monday, February 10
5:57 p.m.

The fellow who worked the evening shift at the Shilo Inn's office started at five. And despite Sally's objections, as soon as he'd arrived Ben and Monique had bundled her into a cab and taken her to her sister's.

Sally might have been certain that Larry wouldn't harm her if he returned, but Ben wasn't taking any chances. And even though they hadn't told the night man where she was going, ensuring he couldn't relay the information to Larry, Ben had gotten the sister's number so he could call later and check that all was well.

While Monique walked Sally to the door, carrying her hastily packed suitcase, Ben gazed at the house from the taxi—wondering exactly how many relatives he had that he'd never known about.

With any luck, he'd meet most of them some day. But only if he could figure out how to get the name he so desperately needed from Danny Dupray without ending up dead in the process.

There was no longer any choice about approaching the sleazoid again—regardless of how dangerous it would be. Because if Dupray had been Larry's contact in New Orleans, he *definitely* knew who'd been behind the murders.

Ben glanced back at the house as its front door opened and a woman who looked a lot like Sally appeared in the doorway.

He could see her exclaiming about Sally's arm. Then Sally said something to her about Monique. When Sally finally turned and waved goodbye to him, he got that tight feeling in his throat again.

As the door closed behind her, he forced his thoughts to the issue of how he was going to convince Monique to sit on the sidelines for what she'd referred to as the final act.

Getting this fresh lead, after he'd figured all hope was gone, meant he still had a chance for a future with her. And there was no way he was going to let her take any further risks—especially when it came to Dupray. But she was so damn stubborn...

Watching her hurry the last few feet back to the taxi, he told himself it wasn't stubbornness as much as determination to help him. And he loved her for it—as well as for a million other things.

"McCarran," he told the cabbie as she climbed into the back beside him. "And we're in a hurry, so I'll double the fare and cover a ticket if you get one."

"You're on," the man said, quickly pulling away from the curb.

When Ben put his arm around Monique, she snuggled against him. "We'll make it there in time?"

"We should be fine." He'd checked with the airlines while they'd been waiting for the night man to show, and had booked them on Delta's next direct flight to New Orleans.

"Ben?" she murmured quietly enough that the driver couldn't hear. "Is there any chance that Danny Dupray himself was behind the murders?"

He shook his head. "No, Danny doesn't have the brains to plan things. He's a middle-man, an informer for whoever's paying, a parasite. The odd time, though, he'll get involved in something if the price is right. So I can imagine his being Larry's contact. But he wasn't the main man. That had to be either somebody with a major grudge against my father, or somebody who'd benefit from his death."

"And that would be?"

"Other members of the Dixie Mafia. Whenever there's a shake-up, the positioning of the families changes. And when it's a planned shake-up like that one, whoever planned it—whoever had advance knowledge, so to speak—usually comes out a winner."

"So who came out a winner after your father was killed?"

"Well...it's hard to tell when you're not really involved. And I had other things occupying my mind at the time. Besides, Dominick was my father's right-hand man. And I gather he jumped in and grabbed control of the family's interests so fast that nobody had much chance to take advantage of him."

Monique was silent for a moment, then said, "Getting back to Danny Dupray, even if he wasn't the main man, he'll know who was, won't he?"

"Definitely."

"Then are we going to go and see him tonight?"

"No, with the change in time zones, we won't land in New Orleans until about eleven. And waiting till tomorrow will be better, anyway. On Mardi Gras, there are thousands of people wandering the streets in costumes and masks. If I dress up, I'll be able to move around freely without worrying about anyone recognizing me."

"If *we* dress up, you mean."

He tried to just let that pass. He knew her *we* assumption was going to end them up in a lengthy discussion, and there was no sense getting into it when they were only minutes from the airport.

She was eyeing him with a very suspicious expression, so he proceeded to kiss it away. And by the time he'd done that they'd reached McCarran International.

"We're flying Delta," he told the cabbie. "So the nearest door to their counter."

When the driver pulled to a stop, Ben paid him double and added a healthy tip. Then, their one small suitcase in hand, they hurried into the terminal.

After picking up their tickets and checking the suitcase, they headed straight for security. As they neared the end of the short lineup, they could hear raised voices at the front of it.

"I'm a security officer!" a man was saying. "I have every right to be carrying a gun!"

"Not aboard an aircraft, sir," a woman told him.

"If you don't go back and check it through, I'll have to confiscate it."

"Oh, my God," Monique whispered. "It's Larry!"

Ben's blood froze in his veins as he appraised the man more closely. She was right. His back was to them, but he was still wearing the security uniform he'd had on earlier.

"I don't have time to go back and check it!" he practically shouted. "You heard that last boarding call for the Miami flight. I've got to be on it!"

"He's taking off," Ben whispered. "I've got to stop him."

"No," Monique told him, tightly gripping his arm. "Not while he's got a gun and yours is checked."

"Hey," someone in the line ahead of them said, "I recognize that guy from TV. Doesn't anybody elsc? It's that escaped murderer! It's Ben DeCarlo!"

Suddenly, the area was a sea of sound and motion. Some people were shouting for the police. Others were screaming and running. Larry had drawn his gun and was wildly looking around.

For a second Ben was filled with indecision. Then he grabbed Monique's hand and they ran for cover. Seeing she didn't get killed took priority over anything else.

They whipped around a corner and he pressed her flat against the wall.

"Police!" a man shouted. "Stop or I'll shoot."

Looking back around the corner, Ben saw that Larry had pushed his way through the security check and was charging in the direction of the gates—with a cop running flat out in pursuit, his gun drawn. Bystanders were scattering from their path like pedestrians from a runaway car.

Ben tried to think, his adrenaline pumping and his heart beating like mad. He had to do something! But what?

Suddenly, it was too late. The cop shouted a final warning for Larry to stop, then assumed a firing stance and began shooting.

Larry went down and Ben couldn't see anything more through the crowd. But the cop didn't stop firing until his clip was empty.

There were a few moments of stunned silence, then someone yelled, "He's dead! Ben DeCarlo's dead."

"Everyone get back!" the cop shouted. "Everyone get back and someone call 911!"

"Damn!" a man standing near Ben muttered to his companion. "Talk about being in the right place at the right time. Our coverage is gonna beat every other news team's in the country."

He pulled a phone from his pocket, adding, "Forget our flight, we'll grab a later one. You just get over there with that camcorder while I phone this in. Be sure you get lots of footage of the body, and try for a statement from the cop. And sound bites from anyone who had a front-row seat."

Ben's stomach was turning over. "What do we do?" he whispered to Monique.

"We get on our plane," she said, her voice as uneven as he'd ever heard it. "We get on our plane because there's nothing we can do here that wouldn't likely get you arrested."

ALL THE DEPARTING FLIGHTS were delayed by the shooting, which gave Ben time to phone Sally and tell her what had happened before the story hit the airwaves.

He found the conversation difficult, both because she was so upset and because he was, as well. He'd barely met Larry, and certainly hadn't had any reason to like him. But he couldn't help wondering what had made his brother a killer. And what might have prevented that.

Telling himself he'd have to put those thoughts on hold until another time, he said goodbye to Sally, still wishing he could have broken the news to her in person.

Monique was right, though. The only thing that made sense was to get on that plane and head back to New Orleans.

They had an unexpected advantage now. With everyone thinking he was dead, nobody would be watching for him. But that wouldn't last.

Sooner or later, and he assumed it would be sooner, the authorities would discover the body they had wasn't his—and the cops would realize he was still on the loose. So it was only for the next little while that he was relatively safe.

"Delta Airlines' flight 642 to New Orleans," a voice announced over the PA, "is now ready for boarding."

He and Monique waited until the initial crush was over, then headed for the plane and settled into their wide leather seats in first class. They were all that had been available at the last minute, and he'd been worried about being conspicuous. Now, though, he could relax a little.

Once they were airborne and the hostess served them each a drink, he used a Skyphone to call both his sister and Dezi. After explaining what had happened, and that regardless of what they'd hear it was Larry who was dead, he arranged for them to get some things he might need.

As he hung up from the second call, the hostess reappeared with fresh drinks. When she left them alone again, Monique said, "How are we going to handle Danny Dupray tomorrow?"

Ben took a large sip of his bourbon. "*We're* not. I am."

She merely eyed him for a minute. "I thought," she said at last, "I made myself clear yesterday. I'm not sitting out the grand finale."

"Look, I—"

"No, *you* look, Ben. Larry is dead. Which means there's no way you're going to get a confession from the real murderer. So we've *got* to find out who was behind things. Otherwise, you'll end up back in Angola."

"Monique, it—"

"Listen to me," she snapped, poking him in the chest so hard he almost spilled the rest of his drink. "I love you, so I don't want you going back to prison. But there's also the little matter that I've been helping you. And at this point, unless we prove you're innocent, *I'm* going to end up in prison too. I'll be charged with aiding and abetting or whatever. And I'll—"

"You think I'd ever let that happen? I wouldn't.

I'd swear you've been my hostage all along—that everything you did I forced you to do.''

"Oh, right. And you think the police would buy that? Give me a break! With my wig and glasses, nobody I've talked to has realized who I really am. But if you get caught and my picture ends up in the papers, they'll clue in awfully fast. And I'll be in *big* trouble.''

"No, you'd simply have to get out of New Orleans and—''

"Uh-uh. They'd never just let me walk, no matter how far from New Orleans I got. There are too many people who know I've been *willingly* helping you. Like those detectives I went to see—on my own. They'd say I had a perfect opportunity to call the cops then.

"Or what about Danny Dupray? And Barb, that waitress at the Twinkle? They know nobody was holding a gun to my head when I went to see them. Then, in Las Vegas, we've got a whole list of people who—''

"Monique, it—''

"Oh, no. My ass is on the line too, and I'm seeing this through with you—*every step of it*—whether you like the idea or not.''

He sank back into the chair and took a serious slug of the bourbon.

"*Now* have I *finally* made myself clear?'' she said sweetly.

BY THE TIME THEY LANDED in New Orleans, the news that Ben DeCarlo had been gunned down in the Vegas airport was common knowledge.

It gave Monique the spookiest feeling to hear people in the airport talking about his being dead. Then their taxi driver treated them to his considered opinion on the DeCarlo shooting while he drove toward the Quarter—the traffic getting heavier and heavier as they neared it.

"The day before Mardi Gras," Ben said when the cabbie took a break from talking to yell at some pedestrians blocking his way, "has become known as Lundi Gras. And the city's almost as crazy tonight as it's going to be tomorrow."

They started off again, only to be hemmed in by more people a few yards farther along.

"Hey, there's no sense trying to drive in this," Ben told the cabbie. "We'll walk the rest of the way.

"The Quarter's completely closed to traffic on Mardi Gras," he explained to Monique as they got out of the cab. "And I guess everyone figures that takes effect at midnight."

They made slow progress on the crowded streets and by the time they reached the apartment it was almost one in the morning.

"Dezi's been here," Ben announced when he flicked on the living room light. "Those are bullet proof," he added, gesturing at the vests lying on the couch.

"What are we going to be doing?" Monique nervously asked. "Storming the Bastille?"

"I don't know yet. It depends on what we learn from Danny Dupray. But we need to be prepared.

Come on," he added, heading down the hall, "if Maria's been here, you'll like what she brought better."

In the bedroom, the bed was strewn with costumes; elaborate headdresses were lined up on the floor.

"My mother," he explained, "was never one to throw things out. So Maria probably had thirty years of Mardi Gras ball costumes to choose from."

Turning toward the dresser, he picked up the cell phone and pressed it on. Once again, there were messages waiting.

Monique watched him call in for them, thinking he looked as stressed out as she felt. They'd been living on the edge for so long she wasn't sure how much more she could handle—and seeing those vests in the living room had done nothing to improve her equanimity.

But she knew they both had to keep going for as long as it took, because there'd be no second chance.

Ben jotted down a couple of notes, then clicked the phone off.

"Anything interesting?" she asked.

"Uh-huh. Our friendly reporter, Farris Quinn, left a message for Anne Gault a couple of hours ago. He heard I was dead, and just wanted to remind you I promised you'd give him an exclusive."

That sent a shiver up her spine. Even though she'd been doing her best not to think about it, deep down she'd been aware all along that Ben really *could* be dead before this was over.

"But there was another message," he went on, "that was a lot more positive. Our psychic called this afternoon, because she sensed something more about me.''

Monique's pulse skipped a beat. Maybe Ben didn't have much faith in psychics, but everything Cheryl Tremont had said so far had proved right.

The source of all his trouble had been his twin brother—the relative she'd talked about. And when they'd located Larry, they'd certainly been face-to-face with the serious danger she'd predicted.

"What was it?" Monique asked. "What more did she sense?"

"Well, she said she has a feeling there's something that would help me—if I can find it."

"What sort of something?"

"She couldn't get a clear impression of it, but she's got a feeling where it is. So, look, I've got to go out for a while."

"At this time of night?"

Ben nodded, rummaging through the bottom drawer of the dresser.

"What are you looking for?"

"I saw a flashlight someplace, and I'm pretty sure it was in here."

A moment later, he turned back toward her, the flashlight in his hand. "I figure we'll be pretty safe tomorrow. In costumes and masks, we'll basically be able to go wherever we want. But if we can't get to the bottom of things by then..."

When he simply ended that thought with a shrug, she said, "If we can't, then what?"

"Well...let's face it, the cops are bound to check Larry's fingerprints against the records of mine. And as soon as they do, the entire NOPD will be searching the city for me again. Even identical twins don't have identical fingerprints, so there's no time to waste."

"All right, then, let's get going."

"No, not you. And just before you tell me you thought we were *finally* clear on things," he added quickly, "whatever this is that Cheryl has a feeling about, she says it's in St. Louis Cemetery Number One. And New Orleans cemeteries are hangouts for muggers and addicts. They aren't safe during the day, let alone at night."

Even though an unsafe cemetery was one of the last places in the world Monique wanted to find herself, she screwed up all her courage and said, "If they're not safe, do you really think I'd let you go alone?"

Tuesday, February 11
2:07 a.m.

BEN WRAPPED HIS ARM tightly around Monique's waist as they headed up Conti Street.

Despite the time, the bars were all packed and the streets were still jammed with people. Most of them were simply celebrating the first hours of Mardi Gras, but more than a few would be pickpockets and muggers working the crowd.

"This vest is hot," Monique said. "And heavy."

"Never mind, the important thing is that it's bullet proof. If we run into trouble, you'll be glad of it."

When he'd insisted they wear them, he'd thought Monique was going to back off on going with him.

But he'd been wrong. She had more guts than any other woman he'd ever met.

"How much farther?" she asked.

"We're almost there. It's just outside the Quarter—near Louis Armstrong Park."

They walked the rest of the way in silence, and as they came within sight of the cemetery's walls Ben could feel his heart beating faster. In contrast to the neon brightness of the Quarter, the cemetery was pitch-black. Inside it, there would be only slivers of moonlight and the flashlight to see by.

"The gate's locked," he said, trying it. "We'll have to go over the wall."

He boosted Monique over first, then followed her.

"It's all vaults," she murmured uneasily as he hit the ground.

"Uh-huh. A lot of New Orleans is below sea level. So until they mastered drainage pipe systems, most burials were above ground." And all those vaults and crypts, he thought, absently patting his gun, afforded terrific hiding places for lowlifes.

Unzipping his jacket, he pulled out the flashlight and turned it on. "You carry this." He handed it to her, then unclipped the Walther from his belt.

"You think we'll need that?" she whispered in a frightened voice.

"I hope not." He took her hand and they started forward into the darkness.

"This place isn't exactly small, is it," she murmured. "Did Cheryl have any idea *where* you should look?"

"She said near the tomb of Marie Laveau—which I know is up ahead here someplace."

"How do you know that?"

"Because it's a famous site. Marie Laveau was a powerful voodoo queen."

Monique made a funny little noise in her throat, and when he glanced at her he decided *terrified* wasn't too strong a word to describe her expression. It made him wish to hell she'd stayed in the apartment.

"And do we have *any* idea exactly what we're looking for?" she whispered.

"Cheryl said it was something metal. And that it was hidden in a vault that had the word *pray* or *prayer* or *praying* or something like that written on it. She couldn't tell exactly what it was."

"Aah. Well, there's probably only one vault with some form of the word *prayer* on it in this entire place," Monique muttered wryly.

When he glanced at her again, she gave him a frightened-looking smile. He stopped, overwhelmed by an urge to kiss her. Then an owl hooted and they both jumped.

"Come on," he said, starting forward again. The faster they got out of here, the better.

"Metal," she murmured after they'd walked a few more yards. "Half of these tombs have wrought-iron fences around them. Could that be what Cheryl meant?"

"I don't think so. She definitely said the thing that would *help* me was metal, and I can't see how it would be a fence. That," he added, "is Marie Laveau's tomb. That big stone one ahead to the left."

Monique shone the flashlight's beam on it. "Oh, Ben, it's all covered in X marks. If it's a famous site, shouldn't they be looking after it better?"

"It's not actually desecrated. Those marks are supposed to bring good luck. And, apparently, whenever they're wiped off they immediately reappear."

"Like…magic?"

"Black magic, I guess. That's what voodoo's based on."

"Oh, Lord, I don't like that sort of oogly-boogly stuff any more than I like this cemetery. So let's just find whatever it is we're looking for."

She shakily aimed the flashlight at the vault nearest Marie Laveau's. It was much smaller and dark, with nothing written on it about praying.

They checked out a few others, then came across an inscription that read, *Our prayers are with you.*

"Ben? This could be it."

The vault was another small one, made of marble. Following the beam of the flashlight with his hands, he carefully felt over every square inch of the surface.

"I can't feel anything loose," he finally muttered. "And Cheryl said what we want is hidden *inside* a vault."

"Then this *isn't* it." When Monique turned the flashlight toward the next tomb, Ben heard her breath catch.

"Oh, my Lord," she whispered. "Look."

He stared in disbelief at the inscription captured by

the beam. They were looking at the tomb of someone named Etienne Du*pray*.

Stepping closer, Ben opened the little wrought-iron gate in front of it.

"This one *is* it," Monique whispered. "This one *has* to be it."

The vault was covered with some kind of stucco surface that had crumbled in places, exposing the brick construction beneath. His hands trembling, he began smoothing them across the front. Then he tried the sides. Finally, they moved to the back, his hope fading that they were really going to find anything.

Monique swept the surface slowly with the light, then focused the beam on the bottom corner. Almost hidden by ground cover was a place where a few bricks were visible. "Try there," she suggested.

Ben knelt and slowly felt around the area. When he discovered a couple of bricks that felt loose, a surge of adrenaline swept him.

He wiggled them back and forth, gradually easing them out. Then he cautiously reached into the space, hoping to hell some snake wasn't making its home inside.

"Is there anything there?" Monique whispered over his shoulder.

He touched something wooden. There was barely room to slide his fingers alongside it and manoeuvre it out, but he finally managed to.

"A wooden box," Monique said, shining the light on it. "But Cheryl said metal."

"Maybe inside." The box was about the size and shape that a set of steak knives would come in—and swollen tightly shut by the humid New Orleans air. He gradually worked it open and folded back the soft cloth that was wrapped around whatever it contained—revealing a gun.

He simply stared at it, afraid to even hope it was what it possibly *could* be.

"Ben? Is this what can help you?"

"I...don't know. But it's a Beretta 9 mm. And do you remember from my trial? What kind of gun the ballistics people said killed my parents?"

"Oh, Lord," she whispered. "It was a Beretta 9 mm. So this could be the missing murder weapon."

Chapter Thirteen

Tuesday, February 11
12:59 p.m.

Monique opened her eyes enough that she could see the bedside clock, then sat bolt upright in disbelief.

Beside her, Ben made a groaning noise.

"Wake up," she told him, "it's late." She rolled out of bed and headed for the bathroom, wondering how they could possibly have slept through the raucous sounds of merriment that were drifting up from the street below.

Mardi Gras was obviously in full swing, and they'd intended to be up well before this. But they hadn't gotten to bed until almost four in the morning, and the fact that they'd been running on empty for what seemed like forever had clearly caught up with them.

She dashed in and out of the shower. Then, while Ben showered, she blow-dried her hair and mentally reviewed the plans they'd made on their way home from the cemetery last night.

When he emerged, his gorgeously muscled body gleaming wet, she simply gazed at him for a moment—thinking he was the sexiest man on earth. Then he wrapped a towel around his waist and she forced her thoughts back to their plans.

"Are you sure we're doing the right thing about the gun?" she asked.

He nodded.

"You're sure I shouldn't take it to the police? I mean, if it really is the murder weapon, then it's evidence and—"

"Exactly. And if you showed up claiming to have the murder weapon from the DeCarlo killings, the cops would slap you into an interrogation room faster than you could say Augustine's. Besides, I don't trust the NOPD. There are so many crooked cops on the force that if we gave them the gun it might disappear."

"But you *do* trust Farris Quinn."

"Monique, we've already been through this. I don't know how far I can trust him. But we've got to give that gun to *somebody* for safekeeping—just in case."

She nodded uneasily, not wanting to think that *just in case* was just in case they ended up dead. Even if that happened, Ben still wanted his innocence proven.

"And if I gave it to Maria or Dezi," he went on, "when one of *them* eventually gave it to the cops... Well, it would just get a lot more attention if it came from Farris Quinn. Especially if he wrote an article about it for the paper before he turned it over. Then the police would be forced to handle things on the up and up."

"I guess you're right. So I'd better see if I can get

hold of him.'' She headed into the bedroom and punched his cellular number into the phone.

"Quinn,'' he answered after a couple of rings.

"Mr. Quinn, it's Anne Gault. Ben DeCarlo's friend.''

"Aah. I'm sorry about what happened, Ms. Gault. I was hoping he really was innocent—and that he could prove it. And not just because I'd get a great story.''

"Yes…well, I certainly hadn't forgotten we promised you a story regardless of the ending. But I'm afraid I can't give it to you quite yet.''

"Oh?''

"No, I need just a little more time.''

"You know, Ms. Gault, the more time you take the more likely that some other reporter will scoop me and—''

"I've got something I want to give you for safe-keeping, Mr. Quinn. Something no other reporter is going to have. And it's an extremely important piece of the story.''

"What is it?''

"I don't want to get into that over the phone, but will you meet me at the *Times-Picayune* in an hour?''

"You'd better make it an hour and a half,'' Ben whispered from the doorway. "The crowds out there are ferocious.''

"No, an hour and a half's better,'' she said into the phone. "Will you be there?''

"All right,'' Quinn said slowly. "I'll see you at three-fifteen in the newsroom.''

"The *Times-Picayune*,'' Ben told her, pulling on

his jeans as she put down the phone, "is over on Howard, in the business district. I'll walk you out of the Quarter to where you can catch a cab. Quinn's sharp enough that he might recognize me, so if we want everyone to keep thinking I'm lying in a Vegas morgue I'd better not push my luck by going with you."

BEN HAD SAID the Mardi Gras morning parades were long over and the early evening ones were hours away, but Monique doubted a single person had gone home or to a hotel in between.

There were more people in the Quarter than she'd have thought possible, some wearing costumes and masks, some not. Many of them were so wobbly they must have been drinking for days, but they were still caught up in the exuberant mood of Carnival.

Since she and Ben hadn't had anything to eat, they grabbed some fresh crayfish from a masked street pedlar and ate them as they walked out to Canal Street—their progress at one point impeded by none other than Pete Fountain, winding his way through the crowd with a group Ben told her was Pete's Half Fast Marching Club.

From Canal, they walked over to Gravier where the traffic was semibelievable. Ben hailed a cab, then took the wooden box from beneath his jacket and handed it to her.

"Make sure you tell Quinn you're hoping there are prints on the gun, so he shouldn't touch it. And that he should guard it with his life. No, better yet, tell him it might be worth a Pulitzer to him if he keeps it safe.''

Monique gave Ben a long kiss, then climbed into the taxi. Looking back at him as the cab pulled away, she tried not to think about what would happen if it turned out they were trusting Farris Quinn when they shouldn't.

By the time she reached the *Times-Picayune* it was a few minutes after three-fifteen, so she hurried into the building and got directions from the security guard who had her sign in.

Quinn, a rough-around-the-edges type in his mid-thirties, was waiting in the newsroom. He flashed his photo ID at her, his eyes not leaving her face. And even though she was wearing her wig and glasses, she had the uneasy feeling that he was sure he'd seen her before—and was trying to figure out where.

Finally, he focused on the box she was clutching to her chest. ''That's what you want me to look after for you?'' he asked.

Glancing around, she didn't see anyone else who seemed even remotely interested in their conversation. ''Yes,'' she said quietly.

''What is it?''

She took a deep breath. ''It's a gun. A Beretta 9 mm. And I think it's the weapon that was used to kill Bethany and Antonio DeCarlo.''

''Really,'' Quinn said evenly. ''And what makes you think that?''

''Mr. Quinn, I can't go into the details right now. Please just keep it safe. And don't touch it in case there are fingerprints. And if anything happens to us, hand it over to the police. But before you do, make sure there's enough publicity that they can't just turn a blind eye.''

"Us," he said.

"Excuse me?"

"You said if anything happens to *us*.''

Her heart began to hammer and she could feel her face growing warm.

"Was that *really* Ben DeCarlo they killed last night?''

She simply nodded, afraid to say anything more in case she made another slip.

Quinn eyed her suspiciously. "How did you get hold of the gun?''

Now what did she say? That a psychic had led them to it?

"I got a tip about where it was," she settled on.

"And where was it?'' When she hesitated, he added, "If I turn it over to the police, and you expect them to follow up, it would help if they knew.''

Thinking rapidly, she decided that made sense. "It was in St. Louis Cemetery Number One. Hidden in a back corner of the vault of a man named Etienne Dupray.''

"Dupray," Quinn repeated, his expression telling her he knew the name—and making her terrified that she'd told him too much.

"I'll call you again," she said, handing him the box and taking a backward step.

"I'm counting on that. And, Ms. Gault?''

"Yes?''

"Don't get yourself killed.''

She forced a smile. "I'll do my best not to." When she turned away, her glance flickered to another man who was standing beside a nearby desk.

He hadn't been there a few minutes ago, and she couldn't help wondering if he'd overheard anything. Telling herself she was getting truly paranoid, she headed out into the afternoon sunlight.

5:02 p.m.

"YOU SHAVED OFF YOUR beard," Monique said the moment she walked into the apartment.

Ben nodded. "I won't need it if I'm wearing a mask."

She removed her glasses and pulled off her wig, shaking her hair loose—aware there was a mile-wide gap in that logic. "But what if we don't manage to get what we need tonight?" she finally asked.

He looped his arms around her waist and pulled her close. "We're going to. I can feel it in my bones." When he smiled, she couldn't make herself smile back.

"But what if we *don't?* Your beard was a good disguise and—"

"Shh," he whispered, pressing his fingers against her lips. "I won't be needing a disguise after tonight, because one way or another this is going to be over. Either we find out what we need to know, or we get the hell out of New Orleans. Like I said last night, as soon as the cops realize I'm not actually dead, they'll start tearing this city apart again. And we can't be here if they do."

"So where will we be?"

"I've already booked us two flights out. They leave a little after midnight." He kissed the top of her head, then took her hand. "Come on. You've got to decide which costume to wear."

"No…wait a minute. Two *flights?* You mean two seats on the *same* flight, don't you?"

"Not exactly. I booked you to Seattle so you can see your parents. Then, once I get settled some-where… Hey, everything will work out. Besides, we *are* going to wrap things up tonight, which makes this discussion irrelevant."

She stood stock still, her thoughts racing. She knew exactly how his mind worked. And he had some ab-surd idea—which *he,* no doubt, considered *gallant*—that he shouldn't drag her off to live the rest of her life in hiding with him.

Well, if he figured he was going to call that shot he had another think coming—and she was just about to tell him so when she thought better of it.

As he'd said, if they wrapped things up tonight this discussion was irrelevant. And they didn't have time to waste on irrelevancies. So she'd hold off on setting him straight until she was certain it was necessary.

"Your costume?" he reminded her.

When they'd finally gotten home last night, they'd simply shoved all the costumes Maria had brought off the bed and onto the floor. But now, she noticed when she followed him into the bedroom, there was a go-rilla suit hanging from the top of the closet door.

It was hardly a standard issue one, though. The fur was white and the beast was wearing red-and-white striped pants, a large red-and-white polka-dot bow tie and a red sequined vest.

"You're dressing up as a flashy albino gorilla?"

"You ain't seen nothing yet." Reaching down behind the end of the bed, Ben produced a furry white head, complete with a floppy red cap covered in buttons.

"You don't think you're going to be a tad conspicuous?"

He gave her a wry look. "This is Mardi Gras. It's the people who *don't* look outlandish who are conspicuous. Besides, I like his face and I can wear the bullet-proof vest underneath without anyone noticing it. You'd better consider that too. And find a costume with a pocket for your gun."

Trying not to think about the need for either the vest or the gun, she started picking through the costumes—ruling out the skimpy ones like the French maid's outfit and the cocktail waitress number—and finally coming across a Kermit the Frog knockoff.

"What do you think?" she said, holding it up.

"Terrific. Lime green's definitely your color."

As Ben finished speaking, someone knocked on the door.

"Are you expecting Dezi or Maria?" she asked anxiously.

Shaking his head, he grabbed a mask from the bed and headed out of the room—Monique on his heels.

When they reached the door he checked the peephole, then said, "Yeah?"

"I'm looking for Anne Gault," a man replied.

"Nobody here by that name." He stepped away from the door, motioning Monique to look out.

Her heart doing double time, she looked. Her heart began beating faster yet.

"You know which apartment she's in?" the man asked. "I'm sure she lives in this building. Nice-looking woman with straight, dark hair?"

"Sorry," Ben said. "I've never seen her."

As the man turned to go, Monique whispered, "He's someone from the *Times-Picayune!* I was worried that he overheard part of what I told Farris Quinn about the gun."

"Dammit, he must have. Then he followed you, so he knows you're in the building but not which apartment. How did he get your name, though?"

"I don't know. Asked Quinn, maybe?"

"No, Quinn wouldn't have—"

"Oh, I know. I had to sign in with Security, so he probably just checked the book. But why did he follow me? Is he a reporter trying to scoop Quinn, or what?"

Ben shook his head and motioned for her to be quiet. Then, hiding his face with the mask he'd grabbed, he cracked the door open and peered out.

When he closed it and turned to her again, he'd grown pale.

"What's wrong?"

"Our guy's standing at the end of the hall talking to someone on a cellular. Which means we've got to get out of here. If he *did* hear you telling Quinn about that gun... Well, there are people on both sides of the law who'd pay him for the information. And I'll bet they'd love to talk to you about what else you know, too.''

They threw on the bullet-proof vests and got into their costumes in no time flat. Ben handed her the purse she'd used for their trip to Vegas, but a glance in the mirror told her that a frog with a huge purse looked downright ridiculous.

When she said that, though, Ben shook his head. ''We'll want the tape recorder. Hell, if we had any more clothesline, I'd stick that in, too.''

Putting his Walther into one pocket of his costume and the cellular into the other, he pulled on the gorilla head, then said, ''Okay, let's blow this joint.''

Cautiously opening the door, he checked the hall. ''Coast's clear. But if that guy's watching the building we don't want him to notice us leaving, so we'll use the back door. Then we can circle around and see if any company comes calling.''

Her hand tightly in Ben's, Monique hurried down the stairs and out into the back alley with him. After racing along it, they made their way onto Royal where they were immediately engulfed in the crowd.

''We'll wait in that café across the street from the apartment,'' Ben said, starting through the crush of people.

The front of the tiny restaurant was open to the street, and luck was with them. Just as they arrived a couple left, vacating a table that afforded a perfect view.

Deciding they'd better eat, that they might not have a chance later, they ordered seafood gumbo—a special from the chalkboard.

The waitress had barely turned away before Ben gestured down the street and said, "Either those guys are masquerading as the Keystone Kops or they're our company."

Watching the half-dozen uniformed officers push their way through the crowd, Monique could feel her anxiety level rising even higher than it always seemed to be lately.

She tried telling herself that she and Ben were perfectly safe—just a gorilla and his frog friend out celebrating Mardi Gras. But when the cops headed into their building she felt anything but safe.

"What if they break into our apartment?" she said. "Will they be able to tell who we are?"

"I don't think they'd break in. That guy who followed you couldn't have told them much—only that a woman who claims to know something about the DeCarlo murders might live there."

"And that's not enough for them to start smashing down doors?"

"I doubt it. Not with fifteen apartments in the building. But I hope we didn't forget anything, because we won't be able to go back in. One of them will probably stick around to watch for you."

Ben fell silent as the waitress arrived with warm corn bread and their gumbo, then took off his gorilla mitts and reached for his spoon. But they quickly discovered it wasn't easy to eat wearing either an ape's head or a frog mask. Not that Monique could have eaten much, anyway. Not the way her stomach was churning.

"How soon are we going to see Danny Dupray?" she asked at last.

When Ben merely eyed her through the holes in the gorilla face, she said, "Don't even think about arguing. I'm not going anywhere except with you."

"Anyone ever tell you you're the most stubborn woman on the face of the earth?" he muttered.

"Yes. So, how soon are we going?"

"The sooner the better, I guess. Let's just hope he hasn't gone off celebrating someplace."

Ben took the cell phone out of his pocket, along with numbers for the Twinkle and Dupray's apartment scribbled on a piece of paper.

"Here," he said, handing everything to her. "You'd better call in case he answers. He knows my voice."

"Everyone thinks you're dead," she pointed out. "So he'd figure it was a ghost calling." With his gorilla head on she couldn't tell whether that made Ben smile, but she doubted it. His sense of humor had to be worn at least as thin as hers.

She phoned the apartment first and hung up on an answering machine. At the Twinkle she got a person, but it wasn't Danny Dupray.

When she asked for him, the man who'd answered simply muttered, "Not here," and clicked off in her ear.

"Now what?" she asked Ben. "For all we know he *has* gone off celebrating."

"How about that waitress who told you Felicia had the envelope full of money?"

"Barb? I guess I could try asking for her. But if

Danny said he figured I was lying about being Felicia's sister, she'll probably hang up on me, too.''

Ben shrugged. "Dupray's not the type to confide in the hired help, so she's got to be worth a try."

Phoning the Twinkle once more, Monique disguised her voice and asked for Barb.

"Barb, it's Felicia Williams's sister calling," she said when the waitress came on the line. "Remember me?"

"Yes, of course."

"Well, I need to talk to Danny again. It's really important, so I was wondering whether you know if he'll be there later."

"Absolutely. The place is packed, and he'd never trust anyone else to handle the receipts on a busy night."

"Oh, great. Do you have any idea what time he'll show up?"

"Not really. But if you give me your number I could call you when he does."

"That would be fantastic." Monique carefully recited the number. "And thanks so much. As I told you, it's really important."

"Well, like *I* told *you*, Felicia was my friend."

Saying goodbye, Monique clicked off. "We'll be hearing back as soon as Danny gets there."

She held the phone out to Ben, but he shook his head. "If she's calling back you'd better hang on to it."

Slipping it into her purse, she said, "I can't eat any more. So what do we do while we're waiting?"

"I know a place we can go." He signaled for the

bill, and once it was taken care of they headed out onto Royal. Darkness had fallen, but since every light in the Quarter was on, it was almost as bright as day.

Making their way through the sea of people, they walked the block up from Royal to Bourbon Street, which, impossible as it seemed, was more crowded yet. Every second building was some sort of club, and despite the early hour, music was blaring out into the street.

"We don't have far to go," Ben said, wrapping his arm around her waist and snaking a path past two very drunk men.

Once they reached Toulouse Street, they turned north. Like all of the Quarter, Toulouse was a mixture of the seedy and the refined, and when they eventually stopped it was in front of a particularly elegant little gem of a building.

"This is it," Ben said.

For a moment, Monique gazed uncertainly at the arched doorway and the leaded glass and ironwork of the door. Then she noticed a small brass plaque that identified the place as the Crescent Wine Cellar.

"This is yours," she said, smiling at him from beneath her mask.

"Uh-huh." He opened the door. "I wanted you to see it."

Inside, the Crescent glowed with polished dark wood and antique glass. And crowded as it was, there was a more ˉsophisticated sense about it than most upscale bars came anywhere near achieving.

"It's beautiful."

Ben nodded. "The renovation turned out well. But

let's go and say hi to Dezi. I'll bet, in these outfits, even he won't have a clue who we are.''

They started toward the bar, but didn't make it half-way there before the cellular began to ring.

Monique quickly dug it out of her purse and clicked it on. Even before she said hello, the background noise told her it was Barb calling from the Twinkle.

Chapter Fourteen

Tuesday, February 11
7:46 p.m.

By the time they turned onto Dumaine and could see the marquee of the Twinkle up ahead, Ben's heart was beating so loudly he could barely hear the roar of Mardi Gras.

All he had to do, to get the name he wanted, was make Danny Dupray talk. The problem lay in how big an *all* that was. The slimy little bastard hadn't lasted as long as he had by volunteering the wrong information to the wrong people.

When Monique squeezed his hand and he glanced at her, she looked so silly in her frog outfit that he should have found it easy to smile. He didn't, though, because she was his other problem. Or, more accurately, the problem was that she'd been so damn insistent about coming along.

He'd taken one last shot at getting her to change her mind, had tried to persuade her she should stay at the Crescent with Dezi. But she'd been just as stubborn as ever.

"Turn on the tape recorder," he said, leaning closer to her.

Once she'd reached into her purse and done so, he added, "And don't forget, when we get into Dupray's office, do your best to edge over to one side. He's bound to have a gun in his desk, and it'll be better to watch him from different angles."

When she nodded he left it at that, but it obviously would be better for another reason, as well. If she wasn't standing beside him, directly in front of Dupray's desk, she'd be out of the most likely line of fire.

Gazing along the street again, he told himself to stop thinking worst-case scenarios. After all, they were hardly defenseless. But the last thing he wanted was a nineties version of the shoot-out at the O.K. Corral. He simply wanted to make Danny Dupray believe that if he didn't talk he'd be worse off than if he did.

There was a lineup outside the Twinkle, and some hostile muttering when Ben and Monique strode directly to the front of it.

"Back of the line, ape-man," the bouncer told him.

"We're not here for the show. I have to see Danny Dupray."

"Yeah? You got an appointment?"

"Tell him it's his buddy Larry, from Vegas."

"What about the frog chick?"

"He doesn't know her, but she's with me."

The bouncer went inside, reappearing a couple of minutes later with a young blonde at his side. She was pretty, but scantily dressed.

"That's Barb," Monique whispered.

"Yeah, okay, Larry," the bouncer muttered. "Danny says he'll see you. Barb here's gonna show you the way to his office."

Ben had never been in the Twinkle before, but a quick glance around and a breath of the air—heavy with the smells of stale beer, smoke and sweat—told him it was an even grubbier dump than he'd heard.

They followed Barb past the runway, where a large-breasted woman was stripping to "Fever." As they reached the hallway that led into the back of the building, Monique rested her hand on the waitress's arm to stop her. "Barb? It's me, Anne."

The waitress nodded. "I figured it was. But listen, Danny's in kind of a twitchy mood tonight, so watch what you say."

Terrific, Ben muttered to himself.

Barb started off again, leading them the rest of the way to Dupray's office.

"Yeah, send them in," he called at her knock.

"You're on your own," she whispered, opening the door and beating a hasty retreat.

When Ben closed the door behind them, Dupray merely gazed across his desk for a moment—finally giving them a narrow, phoney smile. "Well, if it's not King Kong and the Frog Princess. To what do I owe the honor?"

"There's been a death in my family," Ben said, watching Monique from the corner of his eye. She was already edging toward the side of the office, feigning interest in a cheap print on the wall.

"A death in your family," Dupray said. "Yeah, I

heard. I guess most people have. Of course, most people don't know Ben DeCarlo was your brother.''

"No. There's just you...and me...and..."

The sleazoid nodded, but he didn't bite. This obviously wasn't going to be any easier than Ben had expected. And wearing an ape head that restricted his vision wouldn't be an advantage if Dupray got gun happy.

Tugging off the gorilla gloves, Ben tossed them onto the desk. Then he pulled off the head, put it down beside the gloves, and casually stuck his hand in his pocket.

While he was getting a good grip on his gun, Dupray simply stared at him.

"You look even more like Ben than I recalled," he said at last. "Your hair's different, but aside from that..."

Dupray's glance flickered uneasily to Monique, who'd finished examining the print and was now leaning casually against the wall. Then he focused on Ben again. His suspicions were clearly aroused, but he didn't seem certain whether they should be or not.

"So, getting back to what you're doing here, there's been this death in your family and...?"

"And I need to talk to the man who was behind the killings in Augustine's.''

The silence was palpable. Then Dupray said, "So talk to him."

"I mean, I need to talk to him right now. Tonight. And I don't know where he is."

"And you figure I do?"

"I figure you can find out."

"Hey, it's Mardi Gras, Larry. The *Man* won't want to be disturbed. And he's not somebody whose feathers I'd like to ruffle."

Ben shrugged, hoping he looked at least ten times as cool as he felt. "It's your call, Danny. But before you decide, there's something I should mention. I have a gun—a Beretta 9 mm—that I took from a vault in St. Louis Cemetery Number One."

Dupray's already pallid complexion went even paler. "You have it here? With you?"

"Uh-uh. It's in safekeeping. But if you don't cooperate it's going straight to the cops."

Dupray leaned back in his chair with studied calm. "That would be a pretty stupid move, wouldn't it, Larry? When they'd find *your* fingerprints on it?"

"It's been wiped clean. But I'll bet they'd be real interested in knowing it was found in Etienne *Dupray's* vault."

"Well…coincidences happen. What can I say? Now, if there's nothing else…"

Danny Dupray leaned casually forward again, and before Ben even realized the guy was opening a drawer Monique cried, "Ben, watch out!"

He was halfway over the desk—his gun pressed to Dupray's throat—before Dupray got the drawer fully open.

"Put your hands behind your neck."

"Take it easy…*Ben*," he said, slowly doing as he'd been told.

"Get his gun," Ben told Monique. "Stick it in your purse."

She took it from the drawer and backed off.

"Okay, Dupray, now let's have the answer to the big question. Who wanted my father dead? Who set me up?"

"You're going to kill me if I don't tell you, Ben?"

"You're damn right I am."

"Well, that's one way of making sure you end up back in Angola, isn't it."

MONIQUE WAS SO CLOSE to tears she could barely hold them back. In the movies, the villain always broke down when the hero threatened him at gunpoint. This was real life, though, and Danny Dupray was following his own script.

No matter what Ben asked him, no matter how he tried to trip him up, Dupray hadn't said anything that even gave them a clue. And every time Ben pretended he was ready to simply shoot and get it over with, the weasel would say, "So go ahead and kill me. Because if I tell you who it was, that's what would happen to me, anyway."

"You were involved right from the start, weren't you," Ben said, trying a fresh question. "You had to be if you were Larry's contact."

"*Involved* is a little strong. It was just that...the *Man* was determined to ensure nothing could be traced back to him. So, yeah, I acted as Larry's contact. And I helped arrange for witnesses."

"You what?" Monique said.

Dupray shrugged. "Weren't you curious about why Brently Gleason didn't testify at the retrial?"

"You know why?" Ben asked.

"Sure. Because she discovered she'd been set up

to witness the killing. Which made her figure there was a little more to that hit than met the eye—so to speak.''

"And *you* set her up.''

"Indirectly. I knew she was dating a cop. So I put the bug in the ear of another one of New Orleans's finest, and he arranged for her to be in Augustine's that day. Of course, she wasn't the only one,'' Dupray added with a sidelong glance at Monique.

"Are you saying...me?''

He shook his head. "I've never understood how women can be so naive. You figured the photographer on that shoot you were doing, Frankie whatever his name was, was your friend, didn't you? Figured he just took you to lunch at Augustine's because he liked the place. Well, he took you there because he got a nice payoff. See, the *Man* knew a lot of the restaurant's regulars would be too smart to testify. But a nice, law-abiding out-of-towner like you...''

Monique exhaled slowly, scarcely able to believe Dupray was telling the truth. Yet he had to be. Otherwise, he wouldn't have known Frankie's name.

"But how did you know about Larry?'' Ben demanded. "Know that he existed?''

"The *Man* told me. He knew.''

"How?''

Dupray shrugged again, then said, "I'm afraid I'm tired of all these questions. Which means it's decision time. Either you kill me or you get the hell out of my club.

"But you might want to consider that since you don't have a silencer on your gun, my bartender would hear a shot for sure. And he'd be in this office in two seconds flat—with a gun of his own.

"So, if I were you, I'd seriously think about option number two. If you just leave, you can still take off for some place that doesn't have an extradition treaty with the States."

For half a second, Monique thought Ben might actually blow Dupray away. And for the same half second she wanted him to.

Then he picked up his gorilla head and gloves from the desk, glanced at her and said, "Let's go."

She started for the door, knowing he'd made the only decision he could. He wasn't a killer, and shooting Dupray would have done nothing except make an already impossible situation worse. But knowing there'd been no choice didn't help. Not when they hadn't gotten what they wanted.

As she started down the hallway, Ben right behind her, hot tears were stinging her eyes. Danny Dupray had been their last hope, and now they were never going to learn who the *Man* was or prove Ben's innocence.

When they reached the end of the hall, Barb was lurking. "Did you find out what you needed to know?" she asked as Ben tugged his ape head back on.

Monique shook her head. "But thanks for your help."

"Well...sorry things didn't work out."

"Thanks," she murmured again, glad her mask was hiding the tears that had begun trickling down her face.

THE ACRID TASTE of failure in his mouth, Ben hustled Monique out of the Twinkle and down Dumaine before Danny Dupray could decide to send his gun-toting bartender after them.

"At least we got everything on tape," she said at last. "And he *did* admit to playing a part in things."

Ben nodded, but Dupray had confessed with a gun staring him in the face, which meant it wouldn't be worth much to the police. Not on its own. They'd want the identity of the *Man* as much as Ben did. But he hadn't gotten it.

"Where are we going now?" Monique asked.

"Back to the Crescent." He wrapped his arm more tightly around her shoulders, thinking how little time he had left to be with her. It wouldn't even be until midnight now, because instead of waiting around for those flights he'd booked they should probably get out of town just as fast as they could.

But he didn't want to rush into a bad plan, so he needed a quiet place to think. And Dezi's office would fit the bill—although not for very long.

Dupray wasn't going to sit on the information that Ben DeCarlo was alive and well and right here in New Orleans. He'd call either the cops or the *Man*, whichever he figured would be worth more to him.

And once he did, someone was sure to stop by the Crescent to see if Ben was hiding out there.

"What?" he said, jolted back to the moment when Monique suddenly stopped walking.

"The phone's ringing." She dug it out of her purse and answered it.

"Oh, my Lord," she murmured after a moment.

"Oh, my Lord. Thank you so much. Oh, yes, you can't know how much it helps."

She pulled off her mask and stood staring at him for a second. Then a little smile appeared on her face and she said, "That was Barb. And remember how she knew Dupray called somebody the night Felicia was killed? Because she happened to be outside his office and overheard him?"

Ben nodded, his adrenaline pumping. That smile had to mean they'd finally gotten a break.

"Well this time Barb didn't just *happen* to overhear. After I told her we didn't find out anything, she intentionally wandered down to his office and listened at the door."

"And?"

"And he was trying to get hold of your Uncle Dominick. Dominick has to be the *Man*."

"Dominick," Ben repeated, feeing as if someone had just kicked him in the gut. "What *exactly* did she hear? Word for word."

"Well, he asked to speak to Dominick DeCarlo. But apparently he wasn't there, so then Dupray said that somebody had better track Mr. DeCarlo down— and tell him to call Danny Dupray at the Twinkle right away. That it was concerning an urgent family matter."

Ben shook his head, his throat tight. If Dominick really was the *Man*, he'd had his own brother murdered.

"Why would Dominick have done it?" Monique said.

"I'm not sure. But the obvious guess is that he got

tired of being number two, always taking orders from his older brother.''

"And he put the blame on you because…?''

"That one I'm *really* not sure about. Dominick and I were never enemies. But I'm going to get some answers if it's the last thing I do.'' He hesitated, knowing how much success he'd have if he suggested Monique sit this one out. Besides, the way things stood now, there was no guarantee she'd be safe at the Crescent.

"So?'' he said, half against his better judgment. "Are you up to hearing what my uncle Dominick has to say for himself? Or better yet, are you up to taping it?''

"You mean now? You know where he is?''

"On Mardi Gras night? The only place on earth he'd be is at the Krewe of Abruzzi's Mardi Gras ball.''

9:32 p.m.

THE KREWE OF ABRUZZI'S ball was always held in the grand ballroom of the palatial Garden Terrace Hotel on St. Charles Avenue, and getting from the French Quarter to the Garden District on Mardi Gras night took twice as long as it normally did.

By the time their taxi pulled up in front of the hotel, Ben was sweating bullets—and not only because he was hot in his costume.

If Dominick had gotten Danny Dupray's message and returned the call, he'd know his nephew was wearing a gorilla suit. And Ben figured they needed all the advantages they could get, especially the element of surprise.

He paid the cabbie, then glanced around, looking for Farris Quinn. They'd called him from the cab, en route, because however this story ended it was going to end right here. And the least they could do was give him the exclusive they'd promised.

Not seeing the reporter, Ben took Monique's hand and led her down the side of the hotel, explaining, "They check invitations, so we're going to have to sneak in the back way. But the ballroom's on the ground floor, and the smokers will have unlocked the balcony doors by now."

They reached the rear of the building and cut across the secluded gardens that sprawled away from it. The night was overcast, and the only light they had to see by were the pale shafts drifting out through the French doors of the ballroom.

The first few balconies they came to had people on them, so they passed those by. When they finally reached an empty one, Ben whispered, "We're going to have to hop the railing."

"Good thing I'm a frog," Monique whispered back.

He'd have laughed at that if he hadn't been so tightly wired. As things were, he merely squeezed her hand to let her know he'd noticed she was trying to lighten things, then said, "Okay, take your best hop."

When she grabbed the railing, he boosted her up.

"Now," he said, climbing over after her, "turn on the tape recorder and let's go for it."

She gave him an anxious-looking nod and fumbled

in her purse. After she was done, he took her hand in one of his and reached for the door handle with the other.

"So far so good," he said when it turned.

"Ben? What if we can't find Dominick? I mean, what if you don't recognize him in his costume?"

"I'll recognize him." He had to, he silently added, because his life depended on it.

He pushed open the French doors and they started forward, the music of the band washing over them as they strolled casually into the ballroom.

It was hot and crowded, with the standard array of costumed guests dressed as everything from glittery showgirls to a skull-faced man in black carrying a scythe. Ben quickly looked away from him, trying not to think that seeing the grim reaper could hardly be a good omen.

As the band segued into a new tune, he took Monique in his arms. They circled the dance floor twice before he spotted Dominick and Rose. Dressed in Greek togas and holding masks on sticks at their sides, they were standing chatting with another couple.

Ben's gut clenched at the sudden awareness that he'd be hurting Rose by hurting her husband. She'd always been his favorite aunt. But his parents were dead because of Dominick, which left no option.

"That's him," he told Monique. "The one in the toga."

He could feel her tension as they danced their way closer, and when he stopped she clung to him.

"It's almost over," he whispered. "You hang back

a few yards until we get out of the ballroom, then move closer so the tape recorder will pick up everything.''

She nodded, looking terrified.

"We're going to be fine, Monique." Praying that was true, he put his hand in his pocket and curled his fingers around the handle of his gun. Then, his pulse racing erratically, he moved to his uncle's side.

"Excuse me," he said quietly. "May I speak with you privately for a minute."

Dominick looked at him, then smiled at the gorilla suit.

Ben exhaled slowly. Dominick hadn't talked to Dupray.

"Do I know you?"

"Uh-huh. I did a job for you a few years back. I'm Larry. From Vegas."

Displeasure flickered across Dominick's face. "We have nothing to discuss."

"No?" Ben said in a mere whisper. "Well there's a gun in my pocket aimed straight at you, so let's take a little walk. And if I see you trying to signal anyone, I'll shoot you first and him second."

Dominick glared hatred at Ben for a moment, then glanced at Rose and the other couple. "Excuse me for a minute. This gentleman wants a word."

With Monique following along, they headed across the room and out into the adjoining reception area, then down the hall until they reached a deserted recess leading to a supply room. It was just large enough to hide the three of them from prying eyes.

"This'll do." Ben motioned Dominick into the alcove and took the Walther from his pocket. "Now, where's your gun?" he demanded, targetting his uncle.

"What the hell are you talking about? I'm not packing."

"You're *always* packing, even wearing a toga. So where is it?"

"The small of my back," Dominick muttered. "Hidden in the folds."

"Then turn around. Nice and slow."

Ben found the gun and removed it. "Okay, now turn toward me again."

"Larry, what the hell is this about? You got well paid for what you did. End of story."

Ben glanced at Monique, making sure she and the tape recorder were close enough. "Cover him for a second," he said.

Once she'd pulled the snubby out of her pocket and aimed it at Dominick, Ben took off the gorilla head.

"I'm Ben," he said, tossing it down and leveling his own gun at Dominick once more. "It was Larry who got shot last night, not me. And it's you who'll end up dead tonight unless I get some answers. Now, why did you have my parents killed?"

"Are you crazy? I didn't!"

"That's not what Larry told me," he lied. "And it's not what Danny Dupray says, either," he said, adding another lie for good measure. "Or several others."

Dominick suddenly looked less sure of himself. "Benny…how could you even think…"

"Why, Dominick? Look, you—of all people—

know I'm not a killer. And I won't kill you if you tell me what I want to know. But if you don't you're a dead man. I swear it."

Dominick sagged a little, then slowly shrugged. "Your father was a hard man to work for, Benny. He just made me crazier and crazier until…"

"Yeah, that's about what I figured. But where did Larry come in? Why the look-alike? Why set me up?"

"Benny…it just kind of came together. I was on a gambling junket in Vegas a few years back. And I saw Larry in a casino and thought he was you. I mean, I actually went up to him and slapped him on the back. But, of course, he didn't have a clue who I was.

"At least not until I explained that he was the spitting image of my nephew. Then he asked the date of my nephew's birthday, and when I told him that he said you had to be his brother. He knew he had a twin who'd been adopted out.

"Anyway, it started me thinking, Benny. And the more I thought, the more I resented you. I mean, there you were, walking around with the DeCarlo name but acting like you were too damn good for the rest of the family. And I figured… Well, you can probably fill in the blanks."

Anger was ringing so loudly in his ears that Ben could hardly think straight. "How much did you pay him, Dominick? How much did you pay Larry to kill my parents and land me in Angola?"

"Does it really matter?"

"It doesn't, Ben," Monique said quietly. "We've heard enough."

Dominick glanced at her and gave another slow shrug. "I don't know who you are or what good you think this will do you. But Benny here could kill me before I'd repeat what I just said in front of anyone else. And I'll deny I ever said it to you two."

Ben resisted the temptation to mention the tape recorder. He'd save that little surprise for later. Instead, he simply said, "Monique? Call the cops. Then see if you can find Farris Quinn. He's got to be in the lobby or someplace."

"HE SHOULDN'T HAVE TO go back to jail!" Monique clutched Ben's hand more tightly and glared daggers at Detective Marchand—the officer in charge of the police team that had arrived. "He's an innocent man who's already spent three years in a cell."

Marchand paced the length of the meeting room the hotel's manager had provided, then stopped and turned back toward them.

For a moment, Monique was aware how ridiculous they looked, even minus the head of Ben's ape costume and her frog mask. Then Marchand started speaking and her only thoughts were about what he was saying.

"Look, as I explained, it'll only be until the proper documents are signed and the paperwork's processed. But tracking down lawyers, district attorneys and judges at eleven o'clock on Mardi Gras isn't exactly a piece of cake."

"Well why can't he stay right where he is for the moment? Until you track down whoever you need?"

"Because, like everyone else, I've got rules and procedures to follow."

"But—"

"Monique?" Ben interrupted quietly. "It'll be okay. Give us a couple of minutes?" he added to Marchand.

The detective nodded, looking relieved at the chance to leave. Before he was even out the door, Ben took Monique in his arms.

"I don't want to let you out of my sight," she said, barely able to stand the thought of it. "You don't trust the NOPD. And people sometimes have *accidents* while they're in police custody."

He gently brushed her hair back from her face and said, "Hey, I'm not going to have any accident. I'm as high profile as it gets, remember? I'm the front-page story in tomorrow's *Times-Picayune*. And before he left, Farris Quinn made certain every cop within a block of this hotel knew that."

"And you're sure they won't put you in a cell with Dominick and Danny Dupray?"

"No, I'll be in a cell for prisoners on their way out. They'll be in one for prisoners on their way in. And I promise I'll be fine."

"Really?" she murmured, gazing up at him.

"Word of honor." He gave her a long, deep kiss that took her breath away.

"I want you to do something for me," he murmured at last.

"Anything."

"Good. You saw those television crews arriving as we came in here?"

She nodded.

"Well, instead of leaving with me, and being on a TV newsbreak, I want you to stay right in this room and make a few phone calls."

"No, Ben, I—"

"Just listen. As soon as you've done that, you can come down to the station and wait for me. But you can't have your parents suddenly seeing you on TV with a convicted murderer. You've got to call them right now and explain what's happened. Then I'd like you to let Maria and Dezi know. Oh, and you should call the Twinkle for me."

"The Twinkle?"

"Uh-huh. Tell Barb there's a better-paying job for her at the Crescent any time she wants it."

Monique smiled. "You know what?"

"What?"

"You're an awfully nice man."

Ben rewarded that line with another sinfully breathtaking kiss.

"You know what?" he eventually whispered against her lips.

"What?"

"You ain't seen nothing yet."

Epilogue

Friday, February 14
9:45 p.m.

With her arm looped through Ben's, meeting all his friends, Monique was as close to floating on a cloud as it was possible to be within the confines of the Crescent Wine Cellar.

While he exchanged reminiscences with someone he'd known for years, she glanced across the polished floor to where her parents were talking with Maria.

Practically the moment he'd been released on Wednesday, Ben had called and invited them to New Orleans—along with her brother and his wife, who were over by the bar laughing about something with Dezi and Barb.

"What are you smiling at?" Ben asked as his friend moved on.

"Dezi and Barb. I wasn't surprised at how fast she took you up on your job offer, but it never occurred to me the two of them would take an instant liking to each other."

"Why not? We did."

"Oh, Ben," she said, gently poking him. "I hated you because I was sure you were a murderer, you hated me for testifying against you, and when you took me hostage I was more petrified than I'd been in my entire life."

"And now...?" He gave her such a sexy smile she almost melted.

"And now you're fishing for compliments."

"So? Don't I get any?"

"Well, let's see. Now I love you instead of hating you and you don't scare me even a little bit."

"I'll have to work on that, then," he teased. "A husband should be able to strike at least a little fear in his wife's heart."

"Shh, it's not ten o'clock yet." And they'd agreed not to say anything until they'd made the official announcement—even though ninety percent of their guests probably suspected there was more to this party than the freedom celebration Ben had called it.

"It's *almost* ten," he said, checking his watch. "So just before we tell the world..." Digging into his pocket, he produced a little black velvet box.

Her throat tight, she opened it. The diamond was enormous, and even in the soft lighting of the room it sparkled. "Oh, Ben...it's heart-shaped. That's so romantic."

"Well, this *is* Valentine's Day. And I *do* love you with all my heart."

"Oh, Ben," she murmured again. Then she threw her arms around his neck and kissed him—until even the remaining ten percent of their guests must have figured out what was up.

HARLEQUIN®

I N T R I G U E®

★ Cheyenne Nights ★

by Carla Cassidy

As little girls the Connor sisters dreamed of gallant
princes on white horses. As women they were swept away
by mysterious cowboys on black stallions. But with dusty
dungarees and low-hung Stetsons, their cowboys are no
less the knights in shining armor.

Join Carla Cassidy for the Connor sisters'
wild West Wyoming tales of intrigue:

SUNSET PROMISES
(March)

MIDNIGHT WISHES
(April)

SUNRISE VOWS
(May)

Take 4 bestselling love stories FREE

Plus get a FREE surprise gift!

Special Limited-time Offer

Mail to Harlequin Reader Service®

> P.O. Box 609
> Fort Erie, Ontario
> L2A 5X3

YES! Please send me 4 free Harlequin Intrigue® novels and my free surprise gift. Then send me 4 brand-new novels every month. Bill me at the low price of $3.24 each plus 25¢ delivery and GST*. That's the complete price and a savings of over 10% off the cover prices—quite a bargain! I understand that accepting the books and gift places me under no obligation ever to buy any books. I can always return a shipment and cancel at any time. Even if I never buy another book from Harlequin, the 4 free books and the surprise gift are mine to keep forever.

381 BPA A3UH

Name	(PLEASE PRINT)	
Address		Apt. No.
City	Province	Postal Code

This offer is limited to one order per household and not valid to present Harlequin Intrigue® subscribers. *Terms and prices are subject to change without notice.
Canadian residents will be charged applicable provincial taxes and GST.

CINT-696   ©1990 Harlequin Enterprises Limited

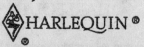

Heartbreak RANCH

Four generations of independent women...
Four heartwarming, romantic stories of the West...
Four incredible authors...

Fern Michaels
Jill Marie Landis
Dorsey Kelley
Chelley Kitzmiller

Saddle up with Heartbreak Ranch, an outstanding
Western collection that will take you on a whirlwind
trip through four generations and the exciting,
romantic adventures of four strong women who
have inherited the ranch from Bella Duprey,
famed Barbary Coast madam.

Available in March,
wherever Harlequin books are sold.

HARLEQUIN ®

LOVE *or* MONEY?
Why not Love *and* Money!
After all, millionaires
need love, too!

How to Marry a MILLIONAIRE

**Suzanne Forster,
Muriel Jensen
and
Judith Arnold**

bring you three original stories
about finding that one-in-a million man!

Harlequin also brings you
a million-dollar sweepstakes—enter
for your chance to win a fortune!

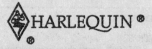 **HARLEQUIN** ®

Free Gift Offer

With a Free Gift proof-of-purchase
from any Harlequin® book, you can receive
a beautiful cubic zirconia pendant.

This stunning marquise-shaped stone is a genuine cubic
zirconia—accented by an 18" gold tone necklace.
(Approximate retail value $19.95)

Send for yours today...
compliments of ◆HARLEQUIN®

To receive your free gift, a cubic zirconia pendant, send us one original proof-of-purchase, photocopies not accepted, from the back of any Harlequin Romance®, Harlequin Presents®, Harlequin Temptation®, Harlequin Superromance®, Harlequin Intrigue®, Harlequin American Romance®, or Harlequin Historicals® title available in February, March or April at your favorite retail outlet, together with the Free Gift Certificate, plus a check or money order for $1.65 U.S./$2.15 CAN. (do not send cash) to cover postage and handling, payable to Harlequin Free Gift Offer. We will send you the specified gift. Allow 6 to 8 weeks for delivery. Offer good until April 30, 1997, or while quantities last. Offer valid in the U.S. and Canada only.

Free Gift Certificate

Name: _____

Address: _____

City: _____ State/Province: _____ Zip/Postal Code: _____

Mail this certificate, one proof-of-purchase and a check or money order for postage and handling to: HARLEQUIN FREE GIFT OFFER 1997. In the U.S.: 3010 Walden Avenue, P.O. Box 9071, Buffalo NY 14269-9057. In Canada: P.O. Box 604, Fort Erie, Ontario L2Z 5X3.

FREE GIFT OFFER   084-KEZ

ONE PROOF-OF-PURCHASE
To collect your fabulous FREE GIFT, a cubic zirconia pendant, you must include this original proof-of-purchase for each gift with the properly completed Free Gift Certificate.

084-KEZ

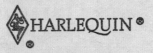